JENNA DIETZER

Dark Offerings

Contents

Content Warnings

Please be aware that within these pages, you will find gore and self-mutilation.

Chapter 1

Em fixed her gaze on the Friday twilight as it swallowed her last employee. Chloe, her hair a vibrant cotton-candy pink, made her way to her car and shot a quick wave back at Em. Her hair bounced for a moment before she disappeared into the night, and Em felt a heavy lump form in her throat. With a sigh, she locked up Sweet Florida Treats, turned the sign to Closed, and buried her face in her hands.

No hard feelings lingered between her and Chloe. Chloe was young and full of hope and energy. But Em regretted the layoff as soon as the words left her lips, despite it being necessary for the bakery's survival. These were tough times. Food, supplies, utilities, and rent dollars drained from Sweet Florida Treats' balance sheet like egg whites slipping through cupped fingers. Chloe was the last painful cut Em had to make.

A calm piano tune played above her head. She'd heard it a hundred times. But in the stillness of the bakery, Em only felt its sadness. She shuffled behind the counter to turn it off. Rain was forecast for overnight, and the sky was already bruised with purples and grays. Its shadows cast across the empty floors and dimly lit marble countertops. Em traced a hand along the cool surface as the remnants of vanilla and lemon danced around her.

She remembered, in the beginning, the bakery brought her nothing but joy, which was only fair considering how much it drained from her. The harsh realities of being the sole proprietor hit all at once—early mornings, late nights, weekends, and the all-consuming roles she juggled daily. It took six months of hard work just to turn a profit. But once she did, she hired an accountant and her first employee, Chloe. Two more part-time hires gave her a chance to move Chloe back to the kitchen and train her as a protégé.

It was a welcome change. Em's own mother had taught her everything she knew about baking. Cherished treasures passed down from her grandmother to her mother and finally to her formed the backbone of Sweet Florida Treats' menu. With Chloe in the kitchen, it felt like Em had a daughter of her own.

However, the reality of managing employees proved to be a constant source of disappointment. It seemed as soon as Em trained one they left, or the honeymoon period wore off. One employee's frequent bathroom breaks raised suspicions of a medical condition or, worse, addiction. "Bathroom guy" had already replaced someone who neglected to lock the store, leaving it vulnerable to a break-in. Another hire, initially charming during the interview, changed his mood within a week. His standoffish attitude and mumbled replies stressed out her regulars and forced Em out of the kitchen to manage the sales again.

The burden of managing her team left Em more fatigued than when she worked alone. Even the accountant had to be let go when Em discovered that a bookkeeping error caused the rent to be two months late. She never recovered the missing rent money.

Even Chloe, with her ever-changing hair colors, tattoos,

and piercings, initially made Em second guess her. But their first conversation shattered all of Em's superficial assumptions. Chloe cared deeply, unlike the others. She followed instructions, arrived on time, and stayed late without being bribed. She allowed Em to lecture her on the significance of using fresh, in-season fruit versus frozen time and time again, nodding in agreement and always patient. After trust was earned, Em found herself behaving vulnerably around Chloe. Whether it was a botched order or end-of-month accounting, Chloe lifted her back to the surface. Em didn't know what she'd do without Chloe, even if she could no longer afford her.

It was just Em and Sweet Florida Treats now, as it had been in the beginning. The cute, quaint space, in its second-year survival mode, still filled Em with pride. White tiles reflected the glow of three large pendant lights above the register. A sliding barn door behind the counter showcased the bakery name with a shiny, vibrant orange in the middle of the word "Florida." Signs and menu blackboards were handwritten in colored chalk. Artificial plants with small leaves like baby's tears sat in the middle of each of the two tables in front of the register.

The display case lights flickered, drawing Em's attention. She retrieved a paper pad and pen from her apron pocket and jotted down *LED bulb replacements*. It might not just be a bulb, she considered. It might be the first sign of a complete breakdown, but that cost was a burden she couldn't bear. She dismissed the thought from her mind.

Em unplugged the unit, relocated her seasonally fresh treats—cheesecake with tangerine slices, a giant raspberry tart dusted in confectioner's sugar, blueberry lemon cupcakes topped with blueberry sprigs—and wiped down the display.

After cleaning and organizing, she dimmed the front lights, returned to the back kitchen, and slid the barn door shut. She had a long night ahead of her. A corkboard adorned with sticky notes lined one wall. Reminders about rent, website updates, internet, insurance, coffee and tea bags. Beside them was an order for 10 strawberry pies due the next morning. Em hadn't even started.

As the wall clock ticked past 8 p.m., Em's face fell into a frown. "I'll be here all night," she muttered to herself.

Then the ringing began. In the corner of the kitchen, a vintage, red rotary phone sat on a stool. It had been her mother's phone, before the funeral. Em took it from her house as a sort of inheritance. Its yellowed cord was disconnected from the wall, but the metallic ring grew louder. Em tip-toed over to it and lifted the receiver to her ear on the fourth ring.

"Hello?" she said into the mouthpiece.

A garble of static poured into her ear. Then a fragile voice surfaced. "There's my brave girl. How was work today?"

Em cleared her throat. "Hi, Mom."

Chapter 2

Em's shoulders eased as she lifted the phone and cradled it against her hip. "It was a weird day," she spoke into the mouthpiece. "I had to let Chloe go. You remember her?" Em knew she would. She'd bragged about Chloe to her mom within a week of hiring her.

"I'm sorry to hear, honey. She was such a sweet girl." The line crackled. "You two are a lot alike, you know."

"I know it," Em admitted. She paced around the stainless-steel prep table. The detached phone cord trailing behind her. She understood if anyone caught her in this moment, they would think she was crazy for talking to her dead mother on a disconnected phone. Some of the former employees had asked about it. Em always told them it was a memento and left the rest a mystery. "You know, I still wish you were here on days like these," Em continued. "I just said goodbye to Chloe then remembered I still have an order of ten strawberry pies to fill by tomorrow by 7 a.m. sharp. It's Mr. Shaw. His Employee Appreciation Day gift to his staff. He just called the order in yesterday, but Mr. Shaw's a regular. I can't afford to turn orders away right now. I need the money."

There was a pause, as if they'd been disconnected. Then her mother's voice bubbled up through the phone again. "Ooh, strawberry pie!" Em's mom had a habit of focusing on the parts of a conversation that interested her, a trait from real life that followed her into death. "Surely you'll be making these with fresh strawberries, yes?" Her mother's tongue clicked, and Em could imagine her face, full of dread and anticipation. It was the same face she'd made countless times before when talking about fresh fruit for baking. The same one Em was sure she'd made in front of Chloe countless times, too.

"Of course, Mom. As you used to say, 'In this house, frozen is a four-letter word!'" Her mom giggled. "So I'll be slicing on my own enough fresh strawberries to fill ten pies tonight."

"And the apples? Don't forget the apple," her mother advised.

Em smirked. "I just happened to restock the fridge with Granny Smiths yesterday. They're not technically in season here right now, but that's the beauty of Florida. You can get all kinds of fresh apple varieties any time of year."

"Well, even if it's not true to your fresh-from-Florida brand, a good strawberry pie requires one grated apple. Otherwise it'll turn out soupy, like everyone else's strawberry pies."

"Okay, Mom. I'm grabbing a pen," Em said, her voice dripping with sarcasm. "I can't believe you've never shared this before."

"Oh, hush!" Her mom laughed that short, snorting laughter Em remembered. The one so contagious it sometimes left them both rolling on the floor. "You know what I mean! If it's not made with the family recipe, then it's simply not worth baking."

Her bias was both genuine and well-deserved. Throughout her life, Em had tasted other strawberry pies, and they were disasters. Overly thick with cornstarch or so runny, it was impossible to scoop out a slice without bright red liquid spilling everywhere. Em's pies, thanks to her mom's teachings, were perfectly scoopable, fresh, and luscious on the inside with soft strawberry layers. They always came out of the oven double-crusted, not open-faced like some oversized tart. Not only did the pies make her customers' mouths water but they also got them talking.

Em sighed and sat on the stool in the corner of the kitchen. "I miss you so much, Mom," she confessed. "I can't believe it was just this time last year when ..." Her voice trailed off in thought. "Anyway, how's it been—" she grasped for the right words— "there?"

Em didn't know where 'there' was now. It pained her to imagine her mother's voice so clearly through the old phone, yet unable to see or touch her anymore. She gripped the ruby red phone tight in her hand.

"Well, it's not like the oceanside condo in Sarasota," her mother's voice noted. "But it'll do."

Em glanced around the kitchen, filled with gourmet food, carefully curated equipment, and pristine steel surfaces. So much care was given to this place in the first few months of its existence, when it should have been given to her mother. She wished for one more opportunity to drive her mom to bingo, one more chance to sip tea on the back porch and guess the birds by their songs, one more real call to the red rotary phone instead of to a ghost, one more visit to her mom's hospital bed the night she passed. Instead, Em was here, filling orders, just like tonight.

Her heart ached. She knew her mom didn't resent her for not being there. In fact, she'd encouraged her to stay and fill orders.

"You'll never have another chance like this, my brave girl," she'd said. "Don't worry about me. Worry about fulfilling your dream. You're the only one who can do it."

Then she died. The guilt and regret and wishful thinking

Em sometimes felt threatened to consume her. Her eyes teared at the edges, and she knew she'd have to end the imagined conversation before her tears fell into her pie crusts. If that happened, she was sure Mr. Shaw and everyone in his office would somehow taste her sadness.

She grabbed a tissue and dotted the corners of her eyes. "Well, I'm glad to hear you're okay, Mom. Talk again soon?"

Her mother's voice faded into her cupped hand. "Always, Em. I'm here whenever you need me."

Chapter 3

Em glanced up at the clock. It had been an hour they'd spoken. She washed her hands, cleaned the prep table, and got to work. Along the tabletop was an assembly line of glass bowls, pie pans, cutting boards, and square green baskets filled with juicy strawberries. She removed the strawberries' pale hulls, tossing the leafy tops into the trash. Then the dimpled skins were washed until they glistened, and Em cut the berries into halves then quarters. She added sugar, corn flour, a splash of freshly squeezed lemon juice, and a dash of vanilla to each bowl. Then she realized she forgot the apples she and her mother had just discussed.

She ducked back into the fridge and grabbed ten Granny Smith apples, which were placed beside each bowl.

Entranced by her own routine, Em failed to hear the knocks on the bakery door at first. But they grew louder and more insistent, disrupting her focus. *No one should be here at this time of night*, Em thought. *It's 10 p.m.*

"Go away! We're closed!" she yelled from the backroom.

The knocks continued. Then a barely audible voice surfaced. "Em? Em, it's me! Chloe!"

Em tucked her paring knife into her apron pocket and wiped her strawberry-stained hands across the front. When she emerged from the back room, a smile stretched across her face. She rushed to the front and clicked open the door lock.

"You're soaked!" she said. "How long have you been standing out here?"

Chloe's mauve hair dripped rose-hued droplets onto the doormat. "I'm sorry to come by so late but—"

"Nonsense. Let me get you something to dry off." She dove into the storage closet and emerged with two fluffy, white-but-stained hand towels. Chloe pressed them to both sides of her head and rang out the rain. "Is everything okay?" Em asked. "I didn't expect to see you for a while."

Or ever again, she thought. She'd do the same if she was Chloe. Write her off and pretend Sweet Florida Treats never existed, except on her resume.

Chloe cleared her throat. "The apron. I walked right out of here with it." She passed Em a neatly folded pile of fabric, with the logo and vibrant orange fruit at the center.

Em felt the lump forming in her throat again. No severance, nothing to reward her loyalty. Not even an offer of a free cupcake every time she came back to visit. And Chloe rushed back here to return an apron.

"Keep it," she told Chloe. "I don't have anyone else to wear it now."

Chloe noted the sadness in Em's expression. "I'm sorry. I didn't mean to make things worse. I probably should've just waited to text you about it tomorrow."

"No. It's the least I can do for making today, well, today." Em shuffled around the counter and grabbed the largest box she could find. "And, here, I know you love the star fruit upside-down cakes." She pulled one out of the display case and placed it in the box. "Please, take it home with you. It's the least I can do."

It occurred to her Chloe was the one who baked the cake she held in her hands. It was beautiful, possibly better than she'd taught her to make. Em stared in awe of it. Each golden star nestled into a buttery, caramelized canvas. It smelled of nutmeg and allspice.

Chloe didn't immediately grab for the free upside-down cake like she might have if Em offered it to her at the end of a workday. Instead, she shook her head. "I can't," she insisted.

"I'll bake another one for the display later this week. Star fruit is in season every month except May and June. No worries."

Chloe reluctantly took the cake from her and placed it in the center of one of the tables. Then she plucked two plastic forks from the jar beside the register and settled into one of the chairs. With the box top open, she spooned through the cake and proceeded to eat as if it was the last cake on Earth.

Em chuckled, watching Chloe chomp through the glistening cake like a wild animal. She'd always been so poised and careful at work. Em wondered if that was her fault.

"What? I'm hungry!" Chloe caught Em's laughter and crumbs escaped from her lips. She waved a hand at Em. "Come on! I'm not finishing this all by myself."

"I actually think you could pull it off if I gave you ten more minutes. But it's late, Chloe. I've got an order to fill. Why don't you enjoy it at home with a nice, sweet white wine?"

Em regretted the recommendation as soon as it left her mouth. She was speaking to Chloe, her friend, not some customer. She thought she caught an expression of sadness sweep across Chloe's face. But if it had, Chloe recovered the next moment and glanced down at the cake. She stirred her bite slowly along the bottom of the box.

"Was it your mom?" Chloe asked.

Em's breath hitch in her ribcage. "My mom?" Her heartbeat raced.

"Why you're still here so late tonight? Was it a call with your mom? On that phone in the back room?"

Em bit her lip until she thought it would bleed, the sudden welling of her eyes betraying her pain. Chloe was the only one who had caught her and kept her secret about the phone. A week after Em's mom died, Chloe noticed the phone's arrival. She didn't question it. But late one night, after Em thought Chloe had clocked out, she overheard Em talking into the dead plastic receiver and peeked her head around the corner.

Em was surprised by Chloe's reaction. Instead of assuming her boss was crazy and never showing up to work again, Chloe gave Em a long hug. Em's hardened exterior cracked like an eggshell, and all her grief came pouring out. Chloe reassured her it was normal to grieve, and everyone had different ways of grieving. People talked to deceased loved ones all the time. She was normal.

Chloe had been motherless for over a decade herself, having lost hers in a car accident. So she knew what it was like.

Sometimes, after a harrowing workday, Chloe would whisper her a reminder to call her mom and talk. That hadn't happened for months now. But Em remembered.

"Yeah, it was Mom. It's been a rough day."

Chloe nodded. "I figured."

She carefully packed away the remaining cake and spoons and walked to the counter to hug Em. Regret washed over Em for the second time that night. She wanted Chloe to stay, but she knew she couldn't. As Em hugged her back, her mind screamed, *I'm drowning. If I could afford you, I would. You're the best thing that ever happened to Sweet Florida Treats ... to me.*

Her mouth mumbled a feeble, "Stop by again sometime. Won't you? I'm going to miss you."

Chloe offered a warm smile and wrapped the apron around her head like a scarf. Then she turned and ducked back out into the rain while hugging her cake. Em dusted the countertops and fiddled with the register then waited a few more moments to secure the front door. Before heading back to complete her work, she extinguished all the lights. Inside the display case, the big, hollow spot where the starfruit upside-down cake used to be illuminated white.

She knew she'd have to deal with it later. Somehow, she'd fill that hole. As her mom had reminded her, for better or worse, she was the only one who could.

Chapter 4

Baking under a time crunch forced Em into the realm of compromises. She considered skipping the addition of apples, given the late hour. Yet it was non-negotiable. She'd rather bake up until the last minute than compromise the way the bake tasted. Instead, she opted to cheat on the latticework because it was easier to fake. Instead of meticulously folding over and under in a true lattice pattern, she would settle for laying out the strips of dough vertically and horizontally into rows. With a little bit of butter glaze and some heat, it would all look the same.

Em could almost hear her mother's voice tut-tutting in her ear, though. "Em, you were not taught to cut corners," the imaginary voice echoed in her mind.

Em pushed down the voice as she consoled herself. *Mr. Shaw won't know. It will taste amazing, and it will still be just as beautiful.*

Rolling up her sleeves, Em grabbed the first apple, pressing it into the box grater until the skin fell away in sheets of pale green. With each apple, she felt her speed increasing. Soon all the apples were mixed in and marinating with the strawberries except one.

Then Em yelped, clutching her hand in sudden agony. The apple core tumbled into the bowl, and with a wet splash, a slice of her fingertip fell in after. Frozen in disbelief, she watched droplets of her blood dribble onto the strawberries. The pain surged through her hand like an electric shock.

"No," she murmured, shaken. "Not now. Not this close!"

She ran for the first aid kit as blood dribbled everywhere. Onto the table, the floor, her apron, soaking through the strawberry stains. Her fingertip throbbed with a pain so intense that she braced herself against the table. Sweat broke out along her upper lip and brow.

The kit had antiseptic wipes, and she knew enough to use them first. But the bleeding made her hands so slippery she couldn't peel open their corners. She grabbed the roll of gauze and wrapped it in a thick, awkward bunch and secured it with a jumble of adhesive tape. Her finger was wrapped so tight her whole hand throbbed. But it stopped the bleeding.

Once she'd recovered, she glanced at the wall clock. 11:30 p.m. She blamed herself for wasting so much time, first talking with her mom then with Chloe. She had a daunting list of to-dos ahead of her: rolling out the crusts, fitting the pie pans, patching the gaps, slicing dough into strips for the latticework, laying the strips, egg washing, and baking. The baking alone was a two-part, full-hour affair per pie. With one oven down since the weekend, she now had only four wire racks available for ten pies.

She didn't even have another punnet of fresh strawberries to throw into a new bowl. If she dared use frozen ones, one pie would taste and look entirely different from the others.

I can't go on like this, she thought. *Down an oven then an employee. Now a hand.*

The possibility of canceling the order sent shivers down her spine. If she did, her reputation with Mr. Shaw was ruined.

Even if she delivered on time but with fewer pies than promised, even if she presented Mr. Shaw her mangled finger, there was no guarantee of his reaction. Would he ever recommend her bakery to others? Would he ever order from her again?

The clock ticked. She couldn't afford to lose this. She couldn't fail now.

It's just a little blood, she found herself thinking, *and the same color as the strawberries. No one will notice.* Then she argued with herself. *It's unsanitary. It's wrong. It's gross.*

Em hesitated over the last bowl of pie guts, caught in indecision. She felt like she was losing her mind. In the corner of the room, the disconnected rotary phone began to vibrate. *Brring-brring! Brring-brring! Brring-brring!* Its bell tone was relentless.

She covered her ears until the ringing faded away. Then she clutched her silicone spatula with an unsteady, bandaged hand and began to stir. She blurred the bowl, blood mixing with berries, and shreds of skin entwined with apple fragments. The aroma of the pie filling masked the metallic scent of blood—vanilla and creamy and sweet.

Em smiled, content by how easy it had been to hide her mistake. She pushed the tainted bowl aside and prepared the flour for the dough.

Chapter 5

The work night seemed endless. But Em got two hours of shuteye, waking on the cold tile floor with her paring knife digging into her hip. Her alarm rang as orange hues stained the morning skyline. She peeled herself off the bakery floor and untied her apron. She couldn't possibly wear it again with the stains. Maybe she should have accepted the return of Chloe's apron.

There was no time to wash, so she redressed her wound with the remainder of the gauze and tape in the first aid kit. Air bit at the tender skin when she peeled back the dressing. She averted her eyes as she doused the laceration in rubbing alcohol.

From the back room, she could see a single car swerve into the empty parking lot in front of the bakery. Even though she intentionally filled the bakery with the smell of fresh coffee, she wondered if she herself smelled as unpleasant. She pulled her uninjured hand through her hair to try to smooth it out.

Mr. Shaw was impeccably dressed in a navy-blue suit and a vibrant red bow tie. It was evident he had enjoyed a restful night's sleep, a refreshing morning shower, and a hearty breakfast before making his way to the bakery. She was jealous. His chipper, almost skipping walk compelled Em to chew the inside of her cheek. A twinge of anxiety crept in.

He's excited. He's been looking forward to this, she told herself. *This is exactly why I had to do what I did. I couldn't disappoint him.*

She'd made sure to unlock the door early, as Mr. Shaw was punctual. His entrance would be calculated to match the time she'd written on his order. No other customer was like this but Mr. Shaw. Most were late for their pickups. Some were very late. But not him.

"Good morning!" he said, stepping into the bakery just as the clock turned 7 a.m. "Are they ready yet? I don't mean to rush you, but I'm trying to beat traffic."

Em gestured to the two towers of pies beside the register. "Right here. I saw you paid online a half hour ago, so everything's set. Need help getting them out to your car?"

"Please," he said, grabbing one stack of pies and Em the other.

The remainder of the workday was slow, with plenty of time for Em to fret. One person visited but only to ask for directions to the nearby mall. She sold two lattes, a guava and cheese pastelito, and her last slice of kumquat pie to a young couple who popped in during their lunch break.

"What's kumquat taste like?" the young man asked, wrinkling his nose. "We just moved to Florida earlier this year. We're from San Antonio."

Em considered. "Well, fresh off the tree, a kumquat is similar to an orange, but with sweet skin and a tart interior." The guy seemed inclined to stick to his original order. "However, my pie," Em added with as much allure as she could muster, "is like a fusion of creamsicle, lemon meringue, and key lime, all rolled into one delectable creation."

That sealed the deal. His girlfriend ordered a slice of the kumquat pie and wouldn't allow him a taste after he finished his guava pastelito.

Em anxiously watched the clock, eager for the moment when she could finally go home and take a much-needed shower. Considering the sparse flow of customers, the idea of closing the shop early crossed her mind. However, there were holes in her inventory she needed to start addressing, like the starfruit upside-down cake. Nursing an injury had slowed her down considerably, and the absence of employees didn't help. She munched on her own overstock and soon-to-expire items for lunch and dinner, realizing there was no one else around to appreciate them. A call to her mother would have been a welcome distraction, but the thought of discussing last night made her feel uneasy.

She needed to get more fresh strawberries. The season wouldn't last forever, and berry items were her most popular.

As Em was writing out another note about produce to stick on the backroom wall, the bells above the door chimed. She glanced up to find Mr. Shaw standing in front of her.

She gulped. "Hi …" A million thoughts raced through her mind. *Someone tasted the blood. Someone found the bit of skin.* She felt her heart leap into her throat and her mouth become dry.

"I don't usually do this, but," Mr. Shaw began, "I wanted to swing by after work to thank you personally. That was the best damn strawberry pie I've ever tasted."

The air rushed from her lungs in relief. "Well, that's good to hear."

"No, I'm serious," he said. His tone changed. Em stepped back from the counter, concerned the compliment may have couched a complaint. "I mean, I've had many of your pies before. I've even ordered this one before. It's my favorite. But something was different about it this time." He eyed her carefully. "Fresh berries? Do you usually use frozen?"

"No, never," she balked.

"Then what did you do? I couldn't place my finger on it!"

Her sliced fingertip suddenly pulsed, as if crying out. She hushed it between her left thumb and index finger. "Secret ingredient." She shrugged.

"Pepper?"

She laughed. "No."

"Well, I didn't come to steal your secret. Unless I could guess it, of course. But I can't." He handed her a business card. "This is why I'm here. It's not mine. It's a coworker's. He reserved a booth at the Strawberry Festival next weekend, but the guy he was sponsoring had to bow out last minute. There's a big competition, a taste test. I think you should call him."

Em grasped the card in her uninjured hand, feeling the heavyweight paper. "I don't quite understand. You want me to enter my strawberry pie in a contest?"

"Well, this year the competition's for shortcake, not pie. But I'm sure you'll do an excellent job. You just need 200 samples, enough for the judges and everyone who pays to do the taste-test and vote." He noticed her eyes widen. "The winner will be announced on the local news and radio. Great marketing opportunity. You deserve it. Just think about it." He turned for the parking lot. "But not for too long," he said over his shoulder. "The guy'll need to know by tomorrow night."

The door clanged shut. Em rounded the counter, flipped the sign, and locked the door. As she strolled back to the register, she read over the card again and again.

The first time she went to the Florida Strawberry Festival was with her mom. It was a cool but sunny March day. Smells of funnel cakes, popcorn, and corn dogs filled her nostrils as they trekked along the browned grass toward the amusement park rides. She remembered the burn of plastic against her hamstrings as she slid down a giant slide, the bumper boat that splashed up muddy water whenever she steered it into someone, the cool breeze at the top of the giant Ferris wheel, the sticky strawberry ice cream as it dribbled down her chin.

But most of all, she remembered red. Crates and crates of glistening red strawberries, the red gowns of the Strawberry Queen hopefuls, the red-soaked shortcakes her mom despised.

"That is *not* a shortcake," her mom scolded one vendor, plucking the bowl from Em's hands. A dollop of strawberry and whipped cream remained on her spoon, and she licked them off. "That's a *sponge* cake. See how it soaked up the juices and got squishy? That's what sponges do." She grabbed Em by the hand and walked her away from the food. "Come along, Em. We'll buy fresh strawberries, and I'll show you what a true shortcake tastes like. It'll put all these cheap snacks to shame."

Em realized, in hindsight, the guy was probably just hired help for distributing the cakes. He didn't deserve the lecture. But, truthfully, it wasn't intended for him. It was intended for Em.

Once they arrived home, Em's mother directed her to take a seat on a kitchen stool and watch as she transformed a pint of whole, fresh strawberries and dough into an authentic strawberry shortcake. The kitchen brimmed with warmth and the irresistible aromas of buttery, toasted flour, sweet sugar, and vanilla. By the time the lesson concluded, Em's mouth watered with anticipation.

Her mother leaned down, positioning the bowl before her, and gestured with a raised hand, signaling her to wait and listen. "Notice how the shortcake layers provide a sturdy foundation for the layers of strawberries and whipped cream? There's a structure to it, at least until you grab your spoon. It's got to be a little crispy, a little crumbly, or it's simply not shortcake. Understand?"

Em understood. She spooned out a large bite and sank her teeth into it.

"Good. Then the next batch is your responsibility." Her mother stole the second bite off Em's spoon, and Em giggled.

A fleeting hope that her mother would call right now crossed Em's mind. She yearned for the familiar voice that had guided her through countless baking adventures before. She needed advice now, to determine if she should compete at the Strawberry Festival on such short notice. But the bakery was silent except for the whirring of the refrigerator fan.

Em tapped the business card against the countertop as she pondered. "You'll never have another chance like this again, Em," she said, channeling her mother's confidence.

She dialed the number, and her words hung in the air as the phone rang.

Chapter 6

Em secured a spot at the Strawberry Festival, and with it, a relentless drain on her time and energy. The wound on her finger continued to complicate matters throughout the week. The urgent care doctors offered no solution beyond wrapping it in a thick bandage and waiting for it to clot over the next few days. They prescribed her a painkiller, of course, but this sometimes made her loopy. So the familiar processes of baking turned into a slow and intricate challenge.

Her pace meant the display case was never backfilled with another starfruit upside-down cake, and other beloved treats began to vanish or expire before her eyes. Having to repeatedly inform customers about the absence of their favorites became an unwelcome routine. It wasn't due to supply chain issues, as some assumed. It was just Em's unfortunate luck. When she showed them her bandaged hand, they always recommended she hire more people help.

After a series of mishaps on Thursday morning, dropping both a fresh pot of coffee and strawberry tiramisu in front of customers, Em flipped the sign to Closed for an hour and grabbed the red rotary phone. Her mom answered immediately. "My brave girl! You kept me waiting. What took so long?"

"It's been busy." Em hesitated. "Can I get your advice?"

"Of course. Baking or life?" her mom asked.

"Both."

"Go on then."

"I promised I'd fill an order—a big order. A competition, really. It's for the Florida Strawberry Festival. But I think I'm in over my head now. This seems impossible."

Her mother dismissed the concern. "Nonsense. It's baking. You can do it." Then she asked, "But how big of an order are we talking?"

"200 strawberry shortcakes by Saturday."

Her mother let out a low whistle.

"Yeah, and it's Thursday already, of course. I haven't had time to restock the flour and strawberries to make this happen. Bakery's drowning, and I'm still dealing with this stupid injury. I'm so slow and drugged up lately. But there was an opportunity. Mr. Shaw knew a guy. I couldn't turn it down. If I win this competition, Mom, it's like the best free advertising I can get. I can convince Chloe to return. Give her a raise. Maybe even hire another accountant!"

"Definitely an accountant," her mother chimed in. "But let's back up a minute. Injury? When did you get injured? What happened?"

Em's throat tightened. She attempted to clear it with a few swallows, but it did no good. Her tongue felt heavy and dry, like biscotti between her teeth. The gash beneath the bandage began to throb. "Oh, it's silly, really. I cut my finger on the grater the other day. It's more of an annoyance than anything. It's taking forever to heal."

"Grater? You cut yourself when making Mr. Shaw's pies? Honey, why didn't you tell me?"

Em's pulse quickened. If she confirmed it was the strawberry pies, late at night after their call, she'd eventually corner herself into admitting to what she'd done after the injury.

"Oh, no. Not then, Mom. It was the day after we spoke. I was so distracted and tired after being up all night, making all those strawberry pies for Mr. Shaw, that I didn't pay attention. My hand slipped."

"Mmm. Yes, I bet that hurts. All good bakers have been there."

"Anyway, I was hoping you could help," Em said, pushing the conversation along. "What would you do if you were in my apron?"

"About the injury? I'd try not to be too hard on myself."

"No, no. The competition. I don't know if I'm in over my head."

Her mother considered. "Which one is more important to you, Em? The bakery or the competition?"

This was one of those questions that cut to the heart of a problem, as her mother has a talent for doing. Em knew it wasn't to make her choose, but to dig deeper and find the question under her question.

Em thought of the dire state of the bakery, how she'd need to downsize or pull back if the coming weeks were slow. But how long would it take to find another space to rent? To move everything? She could nix the rent altogether by baking out of her own kitchen—an option she'd considered when opening the bakery. But how long would it take to regain her momentum without a storefront? Half of her customers found her on errands to other places. The area wasn't bustling, but it had enough foot and vehicle traffic to bring in a few new faces each week.

If she closed the bakery doors to focus on the competition,

then she'd have no customers. No revenue would be generated. She'd be farther down the financial hole. People might even mistakenly think Sweet Florida Treats had closed for good.

But if she stayed open, she might not make it to the competition after all. There was too much to juggle. Then she'd lose the free booth and publicity, even if her shortcakes weren't the competition winner. But if she won, the ticket sales from the taste-testers would be all hers. Cash prize, ready on the spot. That would be enough money to not only justify closing the bakery for three days, but also pay for all the ingredients she needed.

"I need to close and focus on the competition," she finally said. "It's just too big an opportunity, even if I don't win. I had one customer order for Saturday, but she already rescheduled."

She could feel her mom nodding in agreement through the line. "Okay. Competition it is. High risk but high reward. How did I know you'd choose that one? You're just like your mother."

"Mom, please."

"I'm just saying!" Her laughter disappeared into the static and re-emerged. "Seriously, though. You know what you need to do now. Get that flour and those berries and focus on what's most important. And Em?"

"Yes?"

"No shortcuts. Not this time. Thankfully strawberry short-cake doesn't involve latticework. But that's 200 people who will remember exactly what yours tasted like if it wins—and it will! So do it right. Remember, that's the whole reason why you're closing the bakery."

"Now you're making me a nervous wreck, Mom. I gotta go get the stuff."

"Talk again soon?" her mother asked.

"Of course," Em promised.

"Good. There's not much else to do around here, you know."

"I figured. Standby. Maybe I'll call with some really good news soon."

"I plan on it, my love. I believe in you."

When she set down the receiver, she realized her palms were sweating. The large, gauzy wrap felt mushy and softer than before the call, as if it might unravel at any moment. She suppressed the urge to yank it off her fingertip.

Em grabbed her purse and flipped the door sign to Closed. She wondered if she should print a notice for the door, something about seeing everyone at the Strawberry Festival this Saturday. But her mind was soon fixated on reaching the farmer's market for more berries.

The remainder of Thursday slipped away, followed by Friday. By Saturday morning, Em could feel the butterflies pulsing in her stomach. The bakery, filled with the aromas of buttery, sugary biscuits and velvety whipped cream made from scratch, soothed her anxiety. She practiced the assembly of shortcake layers, cream, and fruit for the festival then stepped back to admire her hard work. Each polished strawberry caught the light, sparkling atop the lightly browned cakes. The final touch was a thick, sweet, strawberry simple syrup drizzle, cooked down and strained from a batch of strawberries entirely separate from the ones used in the shortcakes.

Surprisingly, Mr. Shaw called the bakery to wish her luck. He reminded her of the mouth-watering taste of her last pie order and said he was so glad it all worked out that she could take the spot at the competition. "You still sure you don't want to share your secret ingredient?" he asked before they hung up.

It got Em thinking.

She sat two samples of strawberry shortcake on the table before her. Em grabbed one and her spoon and felt it fold effortlessly through the layers of strawberries and whipped cream. A slight push was needed to work through the crumbly shortcake layers. The texture was perfection. She pulled the bite into her mouth with her teeth, immediately sensing the contrasts between cool and warm ingredients. The fleshy berries fell apart in her mouth, and the shortcake softened and melted onto her tongue.

But after she swallowed, the pleasure disappeared.

It was a good shortcake, she thought, but not the best she'd ever had. All she felt was hollow. Something was missing. Her mind ran through the list of ingredients, cook time, and temperatures.

Then her nearly healed fingertip flickered with pain, and she tried to dim it with her other hand. She slipped the bandage from the finger. A maroon drop, as sleek as the rich strawberry drizzle, squeezed out of the scab that puckered along her skin.

Her mother's words danced in her head. *No shortcuts. Not this time.*

Her blood. That had to be the difference. What else could it be?

Em picked at the scab until her fingertip was a wet, red mess. She turned over her hand and let gravity spill the drops of blood onto the shortcake. Then she balanced the spoon with her left hand, dug in, and brought a new bite to her lips. A symphony of flavors burst in her mouth. The original bite had been pleasing and enjoyable, but this—this was heaven. This flavor was what made Mr. Shaw drive back to the store and tell her she needed to enter a competition.

Within seconds, she was hovering her wound over the large

mason jar of strawberry syrup, milking her fingertip until it couldn't bleed anymore.

Em wondered if she had gone insane. Had the doctors overprescribed her painkillers? Had the pressure to make the bakery survive, to thrive, caused her mind to unravel?

Her hand refused to give more blood, and her head felt light now. An eerie and persistent thought crept into her mind. *200 people. Everyone will remember me after today.*

She grabbed a paring knife and plunged the short, sharp tip into another finger. One bulbous first drop of blood fell into the syrup. She rubbed down her knuckles to extract more. This went on for several minutes until her hand grew pale and trembling. The mason jar threatened to overflow with fluid. Em needed to stop.

She ran her hands underneath the tap until the water ran clear. She wrapped small bandages around each fingertip and returned to the table to stir the mason jar. And she stirred and stirred until two shades of red blurred into one.

Chapter 7

Plant City, home to the Strawberry Festival, was unusually hot this March day, even for Florida. Em wondered if this would affect how many people came. She parked her van in the Red zone parking lot then took a tram to the gate. She trekked farther than she'd planned and, still, only a quarter of the biscuits and mason jars of syrup fit in her burdensome basket. She chastised herself for not bringing the whipped cream first, picturing it warming and curdling in the van.

The crowd at the fairgrounds was light but growing bigger. Elderly people dressed in visors and straw hats shuffled around running children, full of sugar, in their bathing suit tops and shorts. The sun had singed the field to brown, and dust kicked up with every sweltering breeze. It was like walking through a pool of warm water.

Em furrowed her sweaty brow and pursed her lips. Her anger simmered at the prospect of making multiple trips back to the van. *Why weren't the baking contestants parked closer?* she fretted.

Hair clinging to her neck, Em followed signs toward the culinary pavilion, constructed specifically for the contest. Her armpits were damp with perspiration by the time she found it. It was an extension of another permanent building that housed goods from other contest winners at the festival.

Em slipped inside the air-conditioned building, seeking relief. She set her basket on the ground beside her and wiped her brow. Rows of ribbon-winning goods were displayed in faux storefronts, wooden shingles adorning the tops and bottoms. Signs above named the categories in bright red letters. Scrapbooking, needlework, jewelry, quilts. The mascots, Mr. and Miss Berry, were making their rounds with their oversized red heads and exaggerated grins. A long table extended from a short, white picket fence, flaunting rows of canned jams and jellies for the judges to sample.

Em closed her eyes and took in the cool air and sweet aromas.

A man appeared beside her and startled her. He had graying hair and piercing blue eyes and wore a bright red button-up that clashed with the pink undertones of his skin. "I'm with the contest. You must be lost," he said. She couldn't place his accent.

"More like biding my time," she sighed. She bent to pick up her basket.

He extended his hands, offering to help her. But she shook her head.

"No offense. I'd rather do it. There are breakables in here, and I want to make sure everything makes it to my booth in one piece."

He nodded. "Fair enough. Then follow me." Em followed his quick stride for a few paces. He glanced over his shoulder to check on her. "What's your name? We need to get you a nametag and find your table."

"I'm with Sweet Florida Treats. Name's Em." She didn't ask him who he was. He would forever be known to her as the man who led her out of the air conditioning.

The heat enveloped their faces as they stepped outside, and he took a sharp left turn. Em's slippery palms made it hard for her to grasp the sides of the basket, yet her grip remained firm.

"I believe I know exactly where your table is," he said.

As it came into view, Em noted the culinary pavilion was rustic and charming. Beneath them was an incomplete dirt floor. But under each table was lush red carpeting to reduce the dust. Above them, hanging fans hung from the vaulted wooden ceiling and spun on the double. *At least there was that,* Em thought. She could hear the rhythmic sounds of chopping, slicing, and dicing, the clicks of photographers' cameras, and the muffled screams from the carnival rides nearby. She set down her basket just as the fans carried the scent of fried dough in her direction. As the lunch hour approached, a few savory and smoky notes swirled also into the air.

Her table had her business name and logo displayed on it. She thanked the man and started unpacking.

"Where'd you park?" he asked, eyeing Em's glistening brow and collarbone. The way he said "park" made it sound like he was from Boston, but she knew that still wasn't right. "There's a parking lot for contestants that's much closer."

"Of course there is," Em said sarcastically. She rubbed away some sweat.

"Park in the Blue lot next time you go out to your car, not the Red. Tell the attendants you're in the contest. They'll park you up front near the handicapped spots. Don't forget to show them your parking stub to avoid double charges."

Em thanked him again and turned her back, wanting to finish the chatting and get to unpacking. But the man walked around to her side and gestured toward her hands.

"What happened?" he asked.

Em felt the pulsating throbs of her fingers below the bandages. "Just a little tussle with my cat last night," she lied. *Who is this guy, anyway?* she wondered. *Why's he being so nosy?*

His eyes remained fixed on the bandages, where some brownish-red blood had seeped through and stained the gauze. Em grabbed a pair of nitrile gloves from her basket and covered her hands with them.

"I tried to pill him. The cat won, obviously," she joked. She cleared her throat until his gaze finally shifted from her hands to her face. "Now, if you'll excuse me, the competition starts soon, and I still need to get my van to the Blue lot. Thanks for the tip."

He nodded stiffly again then turned and left.

What a weirdo, she thought.

After securing a more favorable parking spot and stowing her whipped cream in the refrigerator they provided, Em sensed the lively buzz of the crowd in the pavilion intensifying. Laughter and murmurs of anticipation echoed through the air. Beside to the pavilion, rows of aluminum bleachers began to fill with people. Water stations, garnished with bowls of lemon wedges and unsalted crackers, were strategically placed throughout the area. In the background, a young man with a robust voice repeated, "Testing, 1, 2, 3," his words rising and falling through the feedback.

Em, feeling the weight of the moment, rearranged her table, ensuring the Sweet Florida Treats logo and contestant number were aligned front and center. She scooped out and layered the first several servings of her shortcake. Then, with her gloved, bandaged fingers, she grabbed for the cooled mason jar. Her fresh blood and the strawberry juice were indiscernible. She gave the jar an extra shake for luck then unscrewed the top and grasped her ladle. The dark syrup poured in ribbons as the announcer's bell chimed. People began to form lines at each of the bakers' tables. Em, now fully immersed in the competition, passed her shortcakes to the crowd. Audible "Mmms" escaped their lips, and traces of ruby stained the corners of their mouths.

The blue-eyed man reappeared beside her, this time with a fold-out plastic chair. "Here, take a seat. You look like you're about to pass out." Em hadn't even noticed her own sweat and heavy breathing. She sat as he lifted one of her samples from the tabletop and drew a spoonful to his mouth. The syrup painted along the top of his thin lips like brushstrokes. "Is this your first time?"

Em's fingers tightened around the edge of the table, attempting to ward off the lightheadedness. She noticed a lanyard and badge dangling onto the man's stomach with the Strawberry Festival logo. Below the logo were the words *Official Judge*.

Em blinked rapidly, her eyes widening in disbelief. "Sorry?"

He finished his bite, swallowing without changing his expression. "Is it your first time entering a competition like this?"

"Yeah," Em admitted. "Is it obvious?"

"Only a little," he teased.

He stuffed another large bite between his teeth. It was as if he was trying to devour her shortcake as fast as possible. A wave of panic surged through Em's chest then. She licked her dry lips.

"What do you think?" she asked nervously.

He placed his spoon on the half-devoured sample, wiping his mouth against his red shirtsleeve. "I think," he said, glancing around the lively pavilion, "I will see you at the end of the competition when the winners are announced."

He couldn't have disappeared to another table faster. Em's

stomach dropped. Of course, he'd see her at the end of the competition. All the bakers would be there. What kind of comment was that? She grabbed her water bottle at the other end of the table and guzzled it until only condensation remained.

The judges made rounds, smiling and socializing with the other bakers. She met two others who seemed friendly enough, but the awkward and haunting encounter with the first guy began to consume her. She snuck looks in his direction, comparing his interactions with other bakers to the one he'd had with her. Within a half-hour, she was sure he rushed off because he despised either her or her recipe. After an hour, her confidence waned, and she was certain she'd lost.

His half-eaten sample still sat on her table, a sorry sight, melted and soggy. The whipped cream had flattened, merging with the syrup into a pool at the base of the bowl. *When someone likes it, they finish it,* she told herself. Maybe he could taste that something was amiss. Maybe he knew her dessert was tainted.

Em ran through her mind the judging criteria: flavor, texture, presentation, creativity, and adherence to the strawberry theme. It wasn't too high a bar to jump, but every palate was different. She wished someone had reminded her of this before she closed the storefront. She grabbed another bottle of water and chugged.

"Fancy meeting you here," a soft, warm voice whispered.

Em glanced up. It was Chloe, her smile as bright as the sheen on her rose-colored hair. At first, Em smiled back, but her smile faded as soon as she spotted the red-soaked spoon in Chloe's hand. Her stomach churned with guilt.

"H-Hey," Em stuttered as Chloe devoured the bite. "How have you been? How's the, um—" the word caught in her mouth, "the shortcake?"

Chloe swirled the bite between her cheeks, her eyes gleaming. "The best you ever made! What did you do differently? This is awesome." She took another bite.

"Just some, uh, tweaks to the original recipe." Em pulled agitated fingers through her hair until she made a knot. "But I made this for you before, didn't I? I thought strawberries were in season before you were hired."

Chloe agreed. "It was the first thing I bought with the employee discount." She shoved several more pieces into her mouth, lifted the bowl to her face, and drank down the syrup. "It's the syrup. Isn't it? You've done something different there." She smacked her lips.

Em glanced around the pavilion, wishing she could crawl underneath her table and hide. A crowd began to gather at the center of the pavilion.

"10 more minutes to vote, folks!" the announcer reminded them.

"Excuse me while I vote for yours, of course," said Chloe.

Em watched Chloe march toward the voting booths and disappear into the crowd. She didn't realize how tightly her jaw was clenched until she felt herself exhale. The line in front of her table thinned, and she distracted herself by cleaning up. Once the bakers were called to the stage, terror pulsed through Em's veins. She looked out into the crowd but couldn't find Chloe's face.

The blue-eyed, red-shirted judge stood beside the announcer, along with a young, blonde woman with freckles and a dark man with a mustache. The other judges. The host walked down the line, introducing each of them. The woman had worked as a food critic for over a decade at various national publications.

The mustached man founded and sold over a dozen successful restaurants around the globe. The blue-eyed man was one of the hosts of a long-running Australian baking show. That explained the lilt in his voice that she couldn't recognize. His name was Nigel.

"Breaking news, folks." The crowd fell silent. "Our winner today will not only make local headlines and win a cash prize. They'll also be offered a contestant spot on a new spin-off of Nigel's baking show, filmed in the U.S. for the next several months. It's called Bake Across America, and Florida will be one of the first states featured."

Em gulped, her eyes darting to the faces of the other bakers. Some exchanged nervous glances, a few whispered among themselves.

"Isn't that exciting?" the host continued. "Filming starts soon. So if you or someone you know is a competitive baker, we encourage you to scan the QR code on your way out of the pavilion and schedule an audition. Now let's get on to our winners!"

The mustached man was up first to announce the third-place winner. He spoke highly of the consistency and flavor of the shortcakes made by a retiree. She shuffled onto the stage with some assistance to collect her ribbon and take photos with the judges. She seemed grateful and humble to have won anything. Em wondered what the woman would have done with the prize money.

Next, the blonde judge indulged the second-place winner in compliments about her whipped cream. The contestant was a schoolteacher and encouraged everyone to come to a baking fundraiser she'd planned the following month. Em rolled her eyes over the self-promotion, ready to get on with it.

Finally, Nigel stood in front of the microphone. His voice was flat, Em thought, as if it pained him to be up there, as if one of the desserts had left a bad taste in his mouth. "I'm not one to pass out compliments," he began, "as you may have seen on my show." Several in the crowd laughed. "But the pay-and-scoop booths of strawberry shortcake here can't hold a candle to the—," he paused, grasping for words, "truly unique flavor we experienced from one baker today. Please congratulate our winner from booth 11, Sweet Florida Treats, and its owner, Em."

Em barely had time to think. They shoved her to the front of the stage and adorned her with an obnoxiously large purple ribbon. Then they escorted her to a prop set with a wooden strawberry cutout, green tinsel, and a drape of red balloons. The minutes raced. Her cheeks ached from the forced smile she had to maintain. Her eyes were temporarily blinded by the camera flashes.

When they finally released her, she felt relief but also a sense of accomplishment. The crowd's applause echoed in her mind, and she was grateful she had brought along business cards. Everyone seemed eager to ask questions as she packed up. Where was her store located? Was she really going to compete on Bake Across America? When did it air? Could they put in an order for so-and-so's birthday now?

Anticipation bubbled within her. She couldn't wait to reopen the store. Business would undoubtedly boom. She'd made the right decision.

But a voice inside nagged about how she wronged all of them, each kind word an itch digging into the wounds hidden by her gloves.

Suddenly Nigel materialized at her table and stirred the soppy remains of his shortcake—the only one left.

"Congratulations, Em. Good on ya. Do you plan on baking this for the show?" he asked. "Contestants will be allowed to bring a locally sourced ingredient each week if they choose. It's a risk, production says, but it will make for an interesting bake-off. You'll get more details later, of course."

"Since this one has already been judged a success, I'll move on to other desserts. Blueberries are in season, too."

Em wrung her hands together as he continued to stir the bowl, her thoughts growing louder. *I can't believe you served blood to all those people. It's wrong, Em, and you know it.*

When she glanced up, she noticed Nigel staring at her with concern.

"Sorry," she said. "It's been a long day."

Nigel continued to stare. "You look drained, Em. If I were you, I'd pay someone else to pill that cat."

The corner of Em's mouth pulled into a smirk. "So what did you really think about the shortcake? You can answer truthfully now that the contest is over, right?"

A look of concern crossed his face. He chewed the inside of his left cheek for a moment and stared down into the soupy bowl. "I think the cakes were ripper, the strawberries perfection, the whipped cream a crowning achievement, especially for this heat. But the syrup ..." His brow furrowed. "The syrup was, well, I can't put my finger on it."

He dropped the spoon into the bowl. His eyes momentarily darted to her gloved hands then back up to her face.

"Well, maybe you'll have the words next time we meet," she offered. "That's what they pay you for anyway, right?"

He smiled and gave her a nod. "Boy, do they." Then he turned and shuffled out of the pavilion.

Em took the soupy bowl and dumped it into the trash. As she watched him leave, warm, fresh blood rose up and reddened her cheeks.

Chapter 8

The next week was a flurry of activity. Em juggled her duties at the bakery as best she could, but the intrusive thoughts persisted, and the show's producers started calling and stopping by.

She still had to complete an interview and audition. Being the contest winner wasn't a guarantee of being on the show. But her audition was expedited since her signature bake won at the festival.

Em suspected they'd want contestants who were memorable and entertaining, not just good bakers, and she couldn't think of anything that made her stand out in a crowd. She was just another tired, middle-aged woman who loved to bake. Hardly unique. She got her love of baking from her mother. Again, not unique.

The easiest part of the process was the confidentiality and non-disclosure agreement. Since the episodes would be filmed over several weekends and released all at once after editing, the show's producers told everyone to limit what they disclosed to close family only, preferably household members, and just that they'd be on the show. They couldn't share details about the bakes, wins, or loses. But Em didn't need to worry about this. She had no close friends or family members. The bakery was her entire world.

What bothered Em, instead, was not being able to share the news with her customers. She dreamed of hyping up the event, hosting watch parties at the bakery with servings of each episode's bake ready for purchase. But those hopes were dashed. Instead, she'd be required to close the bakery every weekend, during peak hours, just to film. She couldn't even leave a sign on the door explaining why the bakery was closed.

The gamble seemed too big at first, like closing the store for the festival, only longer. But her mind replayed her last conversation with her mom, how closing for a few days was high-risk but high reward. Then she remembered how it had paid off with new customers from the festival competition and the publicity she'd received. Busier weekdays might redeem weekend closures for a while. At least she hoped so.

The producers interviewed her at Sweet Florida Treats. It was a tight fit for her and five others and a large camera. As the interview progressed, Em could tell they wanted more than they were getting. They asked about her inspirations, goals for the bakery, and the most unique bake she ever created, testing to see if she'd be a good fit for TV.

Each response she gave seemed to drain the life out of the room. At one point, the camera guy yawned and checked his watch.

The lead interviewer folded up her notepad and tapped the pen thoughtfully against her lips. "Well, it was nice to meet you, Em. You'll hear from us soon." Everyone stood to leave.

"That's it?" Em asked, desperation in her voice. "You don't want to know anything more about me?"

"Is there more to share?" The straightforwardness of the question made Em gulp. The lead interviewer offered her a look of pity but gave the signal for everyone to wrap up and leave. "We'll give you a call if you made the cut."

Em sighed. "Look, I know you have other people who are probably younger and more interesting and who are going to be naturals on camera. I know that. I mean, look at me. That's not who I am.

"But what you've asked me so far, it doesn't begin to capture my story." Em peered into the back kitchen. The red rotary phone was poised on its chair. "Look, the truth is I could lose this bakery if I do your show. I've already lost everything else. It's going to be hard to make rent, even with that prize money. I'm on my last few dollars. All or nothing."

The lead interviewer raised an eyebrow and chewed the inside of her cheek. "Go on."

Em took a sharp inhale of air and divulged everything but her bloodletting. Her upstart journey, dismissing her last employee just before the festival competition. She could be their black hole story in a bright galaxy of stars. At least that's how she tried to sell it.

Then Em got a thought. "My mother," she confessed, "taught me everything I know about baking. She encouraged me to start this business, even gave me some of the startup money. And you know what I did to her?" Her tongue became barbed, the words catching in her mouth. She averted her eyes from theirs and tried to hold back the tears. "I left her at the hospital alone the night she was dying. I was here instead, just trying to survive."

The lead interviewer sat back down and listened to her strain and choke on the words that followed, how it started with indigestion and heartburn and the doctors thought it was nothing, how her mom started vomiting blood, and the doctors found stomach cancer markers but couldn't explain why, how she'd declined rapidly but insisted Em should spend her days at the upstart bakery.

"I missed her last call," Em whispered, her voice heavy with regret. "I was busy filling an order, and I let it go to voicemail." Her head bowed, and she shook it slowly, as if trying to shake the haunting thought from her brain. "I knew it was her. She was the only one who would be calling that late. She didn't leave a message, but I wish she had. I wish I'd picked up. Perhaps she was trying to say goodbye.

"The next call came from the hospital, and would you believe it? I let that call go to voicemail, too. My mother's lifeless body lay in a freezer in the hospital morgue all night, waiting for my arrival, waiting for instructions on which funeral home to contact. I didn't find the message until the following morning." A shudder coursed through Em's body. "I hate myself every day for being here. But that's the problem. I *need* to win this competition. This bakery is all I have left."

She watched the crew excuse themselves to the parking lot then gather close and whisper. One of the men gestured angrily and assertively with his hands to the rest of the group. The lead interviewer raised a single finger to silence him. Em turned and started cleaning, her hands wiping surfaces while her mind churned.

Then the lead interviewer reappeared alone, face-to-face with Em at the register. "You're in. One of our casting assistants will contact you on Monday. They'll provide instructions on how to reach the filming location, a general dessert theme for each week, and other pertinent rules. Filming starts next weekend, and a meet-and-greet with fellow contestants is tentatively scheduled for Friday. If you have any further questions, here's my card."

A glossy square of paper changed hands, and Em slipped it into her apron pocket.

Chapter 9

Em arrived at the address provided only to discover a near-empty parking lot. An elderly woman leaned against her car.

"Is this the address they gave you, too?"

Em nodded in agreement.

A golf cart appeared, and the driver explained he was there to shuttle contestants and crew between the parking lot and the set.

"Top secret stuff," an elderly woman whispered to Em. "Name's Irma. I didn't see you at the meet-and-greet last night."

Em clutched a glass jar of fresh blueberries between her hands and feigned a smile. "Em. Too much to do last night. I had to skip it."

"You brought blueberries?"

"Yeah, they said we could. Didn't you?"

Irma smirked. "I can bake with anything."

If only Irma knew what Em had been through last night. She spent meet-and-greet time on the internet, searching for alternative blood draw sites as if she was a diabetic. Her inner calf proved to be one of the least painful and most concealed spots. She drew two short, side-by-side lines. The articles were correct; the pain wasn't as intense as her fingertips, and her skin unfolded into two rich oozes of blood, dripping down her leg. She lifted blueberries from her jar and smeared them with blood until the wounds clotted. As the blood soaked into the blueberry skins and dried, it transformed into a perfect shade of violet—darker than the original blueberry—yet subtle enough to escape suspicion.

Then Em laid out a vibrant, red and purple printed, floor-length dress with a smocked bodice for the filming. No one would notice the wounds when they were hidden by her skirt. No more questions from Nigel or hiding her hands.

Irma didn't say another word to Em as the golf cart sped towards an empty, grassy field. Em felt a wave of fatigue roll over her. It struck her that she had never properly rehydrated after cutting herself again last night. Now, under the too-bright sun and high humidity, she felt trapped.

Em nervously scratched at the bandages on the inside of her calf. She spotted a large tent enclosed by transparent plastic walls erected in the middle of the field. Thoughts of saunas, greenhouses, and rising heat flooded her mind. She if this might be the twist that could compromise their bakes. It was already April, and the temperature would only climb higher.

What idiot thought it would be a good idea to film outdoors in Florida? Em thought.

As their golf cart came to a stop beside the baking tent, the fuzzy outlines within crystallized. Eight bright red picnic-style tables were neatly arranged in two rows, adorned with navy blue bowls, spatulas, and cake stands ready for action. All the accent pieces, from towels to refrigerator doors, were made in red and white gingham. Navy blue aprons lay across each table with the bakers' first names stitched on the fronts.

All around them, people scurried, adjusting cords, fine-tuning portable fans, or dabbing powder against faces. Em recognized one woman, the blonde judge from the festival. Off to the side were three director's chairs with the names Nigel, Omar, and Alice sewn into the fabric.

She and Irma were led to the corner where the other contestants stood in tight formation. Irma broke the circle and started introducing herself while Em lingered on the outskirts, still clutching her jar of berries.

"Em?" a sweet, faceless voice called from the back of the crowd. "Is that you?"

The crowd parted to reveal a head of pink hair, so refreshed in color, it was almost magenta.

Em gasped. "Chloe?" They squealed and ran into each other's arms. "What are you doing here?"

Chloe admitted to auditioning for the show after seeing Em triumph at the Strawberry Festival. She never thought, in a million years, that she'd be selected, yet here she stood. "You brought blueberries?" she asked, eyeing the jar in Em's hands.

"Fresh from the you-pick farm," Em replied.

In that moment, two women hurried over to Em and Irma, fitting them with microphones. One of them gestured to Chloe, who had wandered away. "Sweetie, could you come back and do that again? We may want it for the show."

"What thing?"

"Where you and this lady run and hug each other?"

Chloe and Em exchanged a laugh and repositioned themselves. "Take two?" Chloe suggested.

They went through the motions of the encounter again. Em felt stiff and uncomfortable, whereas Chloe improvised naturally.

"Now," one of the mic ladies said to Em and Irma, "when you're here, you're on mic. No exceptions. Anything you say, on or off camera, could be incorporated into the final cut. You signed the waiver for this. *Capiche?*"

Both nodded. The bakers were then instructed to find their aprons on their tables. Em and Chloe ended up across from each other. The crew conducted a final sound check and directed everyone's attention to the front of the tent. There Nigel, Omar, and Alice stood shoulder to shoulder. They took turns introducing each other in what seemed, to Em, like very scripted dialogue. She almost forgot this was part of the show. They probably memorized the shtick.

Em still didn't care much for Nigel, but she was pleased to see him out of that awful red shirt he wore at the festival. Today's button-down chambray was much better suited to his eyes. Em realized why he had been cast as a television personality. There was a certain handsomeness and charm about him she hadn't noticed before.

The baking challenge for this episode was pavlova. Beautiful, large meringue nests that ushered in summer with a decadent lightness. Em's mind was already contemplating how she could incorporate her jar of blueberries as a coulis or compote. Surely there would be lemons in the tent, allowing her to make a lemon curd as well. But her excitement was tapered by the bead of sweat that trickled down her neck onto her collarbone. This humidity would threaten to turn their meringues into soft, sticky messes. High oven temps, exacerbated by the heat, could also make their pavlovas as hard as a rock.

She wished she could gauge each baker's skill level by appearance alone. It was difficult to discern who might make a novice's mistake and be the first one cut. She wondered if Chloe knew enough about pavlovas to make it through the first round. If she did, it wasn't anything she learned at Sweet Florida Treats. Although Em had made plenty in her time, they weren't on the bakery menu.

Contestants were given the choice of room-temperature egg whites in cartons or fresh-but-cold whole eggs. Two contestants grabbed the cartons of egg whites, a gamble Em knew not to take. While it was true that this could save them the five minutes needed to bring the cold eggs to room temperature, the pasteurized egg whites from the cartons might refuse to whip up to foam.

Em was pleased to see Chloe dismiss the pasteurized egg whites. Maybe she knew more about pavlovas than Em had assumed.

The tent buzzed with activity—eggs cracking, sugar spoons clanging, mixers whirring. Em began the curd first, aware that it would take hours to cool. She warmed her eggs in hot water and used a scale to measure her egg whites to the gram. Then she added sugar and rubbed the mixture between her fingers to ensure it wasn't granular. While the meringue baked, she focused on turning her blueberries into a sauce.

The pavlova emerged from the oven shiny and marshmallow-like, with a crisp exterior structure. Perfection despite the heat. The lemon curd, fresh blueberries, and blueberry sauce drizzled on top only enhanced its beauty. Em was pleased.

By now, she could tell a couple of her peers were in jeopardy. One had a pavlova marked with deep, burnt cracks. Another was nearly in tears as her meringue collapsed under the weight of the thinnest slices of kiwi fruit imaginable.

Chloe, on the other hand, looked composed as she put the finishing touches on her strawberry pavlova. Both were finished before time was called. She winked at Em, acknowledging their strong starts in the competition.

Each baker presented their pavlovas to the judges at the front of the tent. Phrases like "pillowy texture but lackluster flavor," "beautiful but grainy," and "unimpressive appearance with a divine taste" formed the judges' opinions.

Em was the last to be called up. As Nigel plunged a large knife through her pavlova, it gave a soft, satisfying crack. His bite melted in his mouth, and he praised the beautiful balance of flavor between the tart berry sauce and the sweet meringue cream. Alice had equally complimentary things to say about the crunch and airiness. However, when it was Omar's turn, he paused halfway through his bite and grimaced. Blueberry juice dribbled down his chin, and he wiped it away with a napkin.

"Careful there, Omar," Alice teased. "What will they think of us drooling over the very first bake?"

Em stewed. Had she not mixed the blood and blueberries well enough? She thought none of her skin made it into the jar. But had it?

Instead of finishing the slice he'd already taken, he insisted on drinking some water to cleanse his palate and try another. Nigel and Alice both scoffed and teased him.

This time, his slice was drenched in even more blueberry sauce. He chewed and chewed without saying a word.

Em bit at her lower lip until she couldn't stand it anymore. "What's wrong?" Em bellowed. The tent burst into laughter, but Em wasn't having any of it.

"I feel—" Omar lifted a finger as he swallowed. "I feel like this sets the bar really high, Em. However, I sense some hesitancy in this bake."

Em cocked her head and clenched her jaw. "Hesitancy?"

"There's something more you could have done here. I don't know. It just doesn't feel complete. What I mean to say is it's perfect. The temperature, texture, look and feel of this pavlova is all well done. But I feel like you're holding back on us. Just, um, take it up a notch next time. Yeah?"

Em bit the inside of her cheek until blood ran down her throat. He was toying with her like a cat might toy with a ball of string.

They lined up the bakers as they waited for the announcement of both the winner and the contestant who would be eliminated. There were no more tears from the first eliminated. She'd already shed them. And despite Omar's antics, the judges voted Em's pavlova the winner.

But Em couldn't hold back when the cut was called, surrounded by the remaining bakers.

"What does he mean 'take it up a notch'? What kind of a critique is that?" Chloe rubbed Em's shoulder soothingly. "He's just showboating for ratings. I mean, heaven forbid a bake, especially the first bake, turn out perfect."

"But maybe Omar's right, love," Irma interjected. "Your pavlova today was good, but he sees great in you. It sounds encouraging. I would've killed for such a comment."

"Don't call me love," Em hissed.

"Well, at least you won. Does no good to complain after you win. That's like winning the lottery then complaining about the taxes!"

Em turned and stomped out of the tent, with Chloe quick on her heels. She regretted it the moment she noticed everyone, even Nigel, watching her. Even though the film had stopped rolling, her microphone was still on.

Chapter 10

Em picked up the disconnected rotary phone first thing on Monday.

"I know what they're doing. They're setting me up as one of the villains. It's not fair."

"Villains?"

"Yeah. The one you want to root against the entire series. There's always a villain on these reality shows, and it's not gonna be me! I'm not that person. I just can't believe the only constructive feedback Omar had was to try harder. Literally every other baker did worse than me!"

"Did you lose your temper?"

Em's jaw clenched. "Why would you say that, Mom?"

"Only because I know you too well. You were always a bit hot-headed. Just like your mother," her mother sighed.

"Well, I mean, I said some things I probably shouldn't have. I'll admit to that. He caught me off guard. But they were still recording audio." Her face fell into her hands. "I just know this is going to make it into the edit somehow."

"Well, next time he tries to throw you off guard, you'll be ready. If you don't give them any ammunition, they have nothing to play with."

"Thanks, Mom." This was exactly the kind of support she

needed. It was challenging enough to keep the bakery afloat while filming every weekend. She didn't need the added stress of putting her foot in her mouth.

The line was garbled with static. "So what else is new?"

"Not much. I'm just getting a little worried about the bakery," Em confessed. "I noticed a review appeared online late Sunday, complaining about the bakery being closed over the weekend. One star. I was afraid this would happen eventually, but I wasn't expecting it to happen so soon."

"Look, Em. When you're busy, you're busy, and this may all be worth it in the end." The line fell silent for a moment, then her voice resurfaced. "Let's get your mind off it. Tell me what you're bringing to the next challenge."

Em pondered. "I think I'll bring some watermelon. Easy to find. Easy to prepare. Easy to carry to the set."

"Why would you prepare the watermelon?" her mother wondered aloud. "Won't it get soggy by the time you get there?"

Em took a big intake of air. "You know, just, like, cut it in half and wrap it in plastic wrap. Easy peasy. I could even remove the seeds before taping, save myself some time."

"I see. Yes, there are so many desserts that can be enhanced by the flavor of watermelon. And it's unique and early in the competition. Your fellow bakers may never see it coming."

Em chuckled at the thought. "Well, I should probably get to restocking for the week and filling some orders, Mom. Talk later?"

"Of course. You know where to find me. But Em?" Em waited on the line, static looming in the background. "Are you sure you're okay? You don't sound like yourself. I just want you to know it'll be alright. Whatever happens on the show, it'll be alright. You know that?"

"Yes, Mom," Em said. "Thank you … for reminding me."

Em hung up the phone and listened to the whirring of the refrigerator fan.

Chapter 11

The days passed quickly, and before she realized it, Em was in front of the tent again. Her blood-soaked watermelon halves sat on her hip. The crew was already abuzz with talk. Someone pulled her aside before she could make her way inside.

"Addendum to the contract. Sign this," they instructed.

Em could barely read the tiny print. "Why? What's this about?"

"Just some changes to the program today. It's a slight rewording of your non-disclosure agreement. Once you get in there, you'll understand why it was important for us to modify the language."

Em signed, intrigued, and floated over to the other six bakers, who were hushed and exchanging glances.

"What's happened?" Chloe whispered to Em. "Did anyone tell you yet?"

"No," Em whispered back. "They just shoved a new nondisclosure in my face and said I'd realize why later."

Chloe wandered over to Irma, and Em overheard her ask the same question. "I think it's something about the judging," Irma offered. "I couldn't get the camera grip to tell me everything, but he said the judging would look a little different for this episode."

Em felt a twinge of envy, not only because Irma knew more than she did, but also because Irma had already warmed up to several people while Em was being positioned as the outcast. She didn't want Irma building alliances, especially with someone like Chloe. Chloe was hers.

Em shuffled over to Irma and Chloe, intent on joining their conversation. But then Alice and Nigel entered the tent.

Nigel shared the unfortunate news. Omar had fallen very ill since last weekend. They'd carry on without him this week. Em noticed the concern on the faces of the crew and the other contestants. She tried to match them. But inside, Em's heart race at the possibility of a second win without Omar's nitpicking.

Alice added, "Because Omar can't be with us today, we're changing the rules. Bakers, we want you to be the judges of each other's desserts this time. Nigel and I will each have one vote for best and worst bake. Together, your votes will serve as a third judge. So you'll have to bake enough for everyone to have a sample."

Em felt her stomach sink. It was one thing to impress judges with professional palates. It was another thing entirely to impress your peers. She wondered if this would turn into a popularity contest and ruin her chances of a win.

Alice continued. "The baking challenge today is trifles! So, bakers, please head to your stations. If you brought an ingredient you wish to use today, fantastic. If not, we have a variety of fresh and frozen fruits along the back table. First come, first pick."

While the bakers rushed around the tent, Em walked to her table and sketched out the layers of her trifle. Sweet watermelon juice and rosewater jelly as the base, a layer of almond cake, cut watermelon cubes, then cream, topped with the remaining watermelon, jelly cubes, and sprinkled pistachios. But would she have enough of her own watermelon to go around? There were other watermelons sitting with the rest of the fresh fruit in the back, but she'd need to use her blood-soaked ones in all the trifles. Would that be enough blood to leave everyone's mouths watering?

To add to the drama, this time the bakers were pulled into interviews one-by-one in another, smaller tent within earshot of the main tent. They interrupted Em for her interview at an inopportune time, while she was carefully mixing ingredients for the almond cake. She'd have to remember where she'd left off. Too much sugar, and her cake would be heavy and dense. Not enough leavening agent and it wouldn't rise. She tried not to be distracted during the interview, but it was obvious she was. All she wanted to do was get back to her station.

When they released Em from her interview, she and Irma crossed paths. Instead of rushing back to her table, Em hung around the small tent and listened in.

"So this is quite the twist, right, Irma? What do you think of your competitors?"

"Well," Irma began, "I'm sorry to hear of Omar's illness. We all hope he gets better soon. Or at least most of us do. I don't know so much about that Em woman. She was pretty hard on him after she won last time."

"Will this affect how you judge the trifles today?"

"You know, I'm only one of seven votes that tally into what would have been Omar's vote. My vote doesn't count much." She lowered her voice. "But it might affect my vote."

"How so?"

"Well, should Em get to win again, especially when she doesn't appreciate it? It's enough that we're known for the Florida Man headlines. Do we want to be known for our grumpy bakers, too?"

Em decided she'd heard enough. She walked back to her table, her cheeks flushed with rage, and picked up her sugar.

Chloe glanced over. "Everything all right, Em?"

"Bad timing for an interview. I'm just concerned I'll screw up my almond cake now." She peered over at Chloe, who wore a sad frown. "It's okay. I'll be fine. Let's bake."

They had danced through this routine several times at Sweet Florida Treats, with Em self-sabotaging and Chloe coming to her rescue. Here, that wasn't an option. It would make Em look vulnerable, and she didn't want to bring Chloe down into her drama with Irma again. As much as Em craved instant relief, they were on camera, on audio—as if the whole world was watching.

Instead, Em doubled up on tainted watermelon for one of her trifles, hoping she could find a way to pass it to Irma. To conceal the extra chunks, she pressed each layer deeper into the glass.

As they walked around the tent and tasted each other's creations, Em was unimpressed. At least half of them were berry-based and hard to compare—blueberry versus strawberry versus raspberry. Em realized her mother was right about the uniqueness of her watermelon choice.

They were interviewed individually again when they cast their votes. Em gave her ultimate praise to Chloe's trifle, with its margarita-themed flavors. For Irma's trifle, she offered her harshest critique, calling its appearance amateur and old-fashioned. This was war.

Everyone was excused while they tallied the votes. In the end, Irma landed somewhere in the middle of the votes, and Chloe was a strong second. Em came out on top again, and they said goodbye to a younger baker, one who fell into the berry trap and into the background of flavors.

Just before the group dispersed, Irma approached Em, her expression unreadable.

"You played your cards well, love," Irma remarked. "But in games, nothing is guaranteed."

Em wanted to tell her not to call her 'love' again. But there was no need this time. Even if Irma hadn't voted her trifle as the best, her sample glass told Em everything. It sat empty, except for a tinge of pink along the bottom. All that watermelon, all that blood, was sitting deep in Irma's gut. Em got her revenge before Irma even opened her mouth.

"Thanks for the reminder, Irma," she said. "See you next week."

Chapter 12

The following weekend, Em noticed the same high tension among the crew when she arrived.

"This way," one of them signaled. She clutched a jar of tainted blackberries and followed him.

"Another change to the non-disclosure?" she joked.

His only reply was a terse "No."

They reached a trailer, which she'd never seen on the lot before, and when the door opened, she noticed all the other bakers inside. They sat on the couch with sour faces, as if they were waiting to speak to the school principal. All the ingredients they brought were lined up on a nearby countertop.

"We wanted to tell you all together," the crew member explained. "Please, sit."

A space appeared between Chloe and another baker named Derrek on the couch. Em sat down between them. A producer plucked the jar of blackberries from her hands and set it on the countertop with the rest.

"Where's Irma?" Em whispered to Chloe.

"I think that's why we're here. You don't think she died, do you?"

"Well, she was old."

Derrek gave Em the side eye just as two crew members

interrupted their chatter. "Should we film this? We may need it for the show later."

"I'd rather not," another replied. "If someone complains, blame it on me. If someone insists, we can always come back and reenact it."

A trash bin appeared, and with it, all the bakers' fruits were swept away. "Hey! What's going on?" Derrek shouted. He'd been a quiet contestant up to this point. Em was surprised by the sudden burst of emotions. He must've felt as strongly about the ingredient he brought as Em did.

"We've had another incident. Irma's been hospitalized."

Em felt panic rush through her.

"For your safety, as well as ours, no one will be allowed to bring their own ingredients going forward. All the fruit will be provided on set and washed and inspected to high standards."

"You think Irma got sick from something she ate here?" Chloe asked in disbelief.

"The timing matches. She ended up in the E.R. the night after we filmed. Omar, too, got sick right after filming. We just can't take any chances. Don't take it personally," he assured them. "It's not like we think you're sabotaging the food." Derrek rolled his eyes and scoffed. Em gulped. "We just need to take extra precautions so no one else gets sick."

As the bakers returned to their stations in silence, Em became concerned the show might get canceled. She expected Irma to be her downfall, but not for Irma to take the whole show down with her.

The cameras started rolling again as the judges walked through another scripted scene, less humorous this time. Beads of sweat formed above Em's eyebrows and trickled down to her chin. All she could think about were the tainted blackberries that would never make it into her bake. All that blood spilled for nothing. Would she ever win again? Her mouth felt parched, and she grabbed for a glass of water. The cool swig provided little relief.

The introduction for this week's bake, a braided puff pastry, unfolded on air. But Em felt distracted. Her head swam. Her skull felt on fire. She snatched a towel and soaked it in cold water and draped it along the back of her neck. Her splashing made so much commotion, Chloe caught her eye with an expression of concern.

Get your shit together, Em, she coached herself. *Get that flour and those berries and focus on what's most important, just like Mom said.*

Em tried to redirect her thoughts to the task at hand. If she could focus enough to master the braiding technique, she might avoid disaster. They had blackberries on set. A glimmer of hope.

Em diligently mixed and whipped the puff pastry from scratch, macerated the blackberries, and piped the cream cheese. Her creation was the first one in the oven. When it was done, the buttery, golden ribbon of dough burst with tendrils of blackberry jam. She was proud of herself. It was possibly one of her best bakes yet.

The judges cut it into thirds, one for each of them, and commented on the sweet drizzles of color and the elegance of her braiding. One by one they took a bite and chewed and swallowed, and one by one their mouths delivered blows to her confidence. Ho-hum. Average. Run-of-the-mill. Em's heart pulsed rapidly in her chest.

"You're looking flush, Em. You okay?" Alice asked in the middle of her critique.

As Em's knees swayed, she thought she heard a distant rumble, the sound of a train. It grew louder, into a deafening roar, then she succumbed to darkness.

When Em woke, she was wet and clammy, like she'd jumped into a pool. A blur of disembodied whispers weaved in and out of her consciousness. All around her was the rich, buttery fragrance of the puffs. The contours of the baking tent, at first fuzzy, unfolded above her.

"Haven't we had enough drama for one day?"

"Does she need an ambulance?"

"No, I think she just fainted. It wasn't, like, a seizure or anything serious."

"Well, she should at least see the medic. That's why we hired him."

A woman's face appeared above Em. "I hate to ask this," she said to Em. "But if you're up for it, we need to film your critiques again. The medic's headed over. He'll check you out first."

Em moaned.

With an ice pack soothing the back of her neck, Em watched while the other bakers received their critiques. Although she was sure she wouldn't be eliminated, she couldn't help but notice the disparity. Chloe's and Derrek's critiques were glowing in comparison, and by the end of it, Chloe was announced the winner.

Em put on a happy face and congratulated Chloe. But as soon as she left for home, Em was forced to deal with the sticky, heavy feeling of jealousy growing inside her gut.

Chapter 13

"Mom, we have to talk." Em cleared her throat. "Have to talk ..." She tugged at her apron strings and paced the Sweet Florida Treats' kitchen as she tried to figure out what to say.

The sun had long vanished behind the concrete buildings, leaving Em with only guilt-ridden thoughts and shadows. She'd spoken to almost no one that whole week, letting the shame fester inside of her. She was both ashamed she had lost and ashamed she was upset Chloe had won. She was ashamed because her blood had likely sent Irma to the hospital, but also ashamed she'd make the same decisions all over again if given the chance.

Tomorrow was another Saturday, the taping of another episode. Her wounds from the previous bloodletting were healed, but she couldn't seem to shake her first loss. Desperation grew inside of her. She kept thinking, if she could just explain all this to her mom, everything would turn out okay. It always did after she talked to her.

But every time she practiced what she'd say, her tongue felt more like sandpaper.

Em reached for the disconnected rotary phone and dialed her mother's number, the static crackling harshly in her ears as her mother's voice filtered through. "Em, dear? Is that you?"

"Hi, Mom."

"Hello? Did we lose the connection?"

"No, I'm here." Em sighed. "I just—I'm feeling a little down."

"Oh. Well, why's that?"

Em winced. "I lost the baking challenge last weekend. It was terrible, embarrassing . . . surprising to not come in first, especially since it was such a beautiful bake. I don't know why, but I'm worried it'll happen again tomorrow."

"May I ask what they asked you all to bake?"

"A braided puff pastry. Mine was blackberry and cream."

"Mmm. I can practically taste it now. But you know puff pastry like the back of your hand, Em." Static licked across the earpiece. "So what did they do? Ask you all to bake it without flour or something crazy like that?"

"Not exactly. The only real difference was that we couldn't use the fruit we brought."

Her mother chortled. "Sounds silly, but alright." Then her tone softened. "Did you lose your confidence, sweetie? Everyone does sometimes. But your attention to detail, your dedication to perfection, regardless of whose ingredients you use … you're destined to shine again. Even if the judges had an 'off' day, that doesn't mean you can't win this whole thing."

Em fiddled with her apron. "I just don't want to disappoint you, Mom."

"You can't disappoint me, dear. I'm dead."

They shared a laugh, but Em felt tears prickling at her eyes. "Hey, Mom?" she started, but couldn't bring herself to say more.

"Yes? Something weighing on you, Em? You know you can tell me anything."

Em took a deep breath. "Mom, I've been keeping a secret

from you, and it's tearing me apart. I don't know how I let it get this far. You know that night I didn't pick up the phone? That rush order of strawberry pies for Mr. Shaw?"

"Yes, of course."

"Well, I did something awful that night. I cut my finger, and blood got into the pie. But I didn't have enough time or ingredients to fix it. So I just gave it to him that way. Then you know what happened? He loved it. And I got this idea I should add some blood to my strawberry shortcakes for the festival, too. Not much. Just a little. It was only a few drops. Then I won that, too.

"Then the baking show started, and with the stakes so high, I thought I should keep doing it. I kept adding blood to my fruit and syrups, and I kept winning. But when they said we couldn't bring our own stuff anymore, for the braided pastries, I lost." She caught her breath, and the phone clicked against her ear. "I never intended to hurt anyone. I just got carried away. Is this making any sense?"

The wait for her mother's response was agonizing.

"You've always had such talent and skill, Em. Why would you stoop to this? You can't possibly believe tainting food with your blood is what made you win all those times."

Em was in shock. "But I do. I absolutely do. It's the only thing that makes sense. How else would you explain this winning streak?"

"Talent!" her mother yelled into the receiver. Em jumped back. "Don't you realize the consequences of your actions? It's not just about winning the competition. It's about saving your bakery and your reputation and your craft. But if anyone finds out what you did, you could destroy all of that. This goes against everything I taught you, Em, everything we stand for!"

We. The word grated in Em's ears and tightened her stomach. It was worse than hearing her mom was disappointed, worse than her hanging up the phone in anger. Em felt a warm, bitter taste flood her mouth and realized she'd bitten her own tongue.

"Oh, Em! How could you?"

Through the line, Em heard her mother burst into sobs. Em's heart shattered in her chest as the crying intensified.

"Please don't be mad at me," Em begged. "I'm sorry. I'll do better. I promise. It was a mistake. I know that now. It won't happen again, Mom." She waited. "Mom?"

When the line stayed silent, Em's panic overtook her.

"Mom? Mom? Are you there? Did I lose you?"

A soft sob bubbled up from the receiver and faded away. Then static overtook the line, washing her mother's voice to nothing, like water down a drain.

Em felt herself hyperventilating. "Mommy!"

Chapter 14

The bright morning sun stung Em's swollen eyes as a crew member chauffeured her to the field. Upon catching sight of her, the makeup artist muttered, "Shit."

Em frowned as the disgruntled man applied ice cubes under her eyes and berated her for showing up in such a state. Em stared down at her new blue A-line dress and the sleek black scarf she'd wrapped around her neck, realizing how futile it was to get dolled up if her face gave her misery away.

"What happened? A breakup? Someone in the family die?" the makeup artist prodded. His concern made Em tear up again. "No, no. I shouldn't have asked. Just focus on the beautiful, sunny day ahead and how you'll shine in this episode.

Your attention to detail, your dedication to perfection ... you're destined to shine again.

It was all Em could do to keep it together. The makeup artist walked her through a breathing exercise and did everything he could to calm her down. After her face was fixed and her mind numb, Em searched for the other bakers.

Irma was nowhere in sight.

"She's recovering," a producer explained when Em asked. "But she declined our offer to return to the show. It took a lot out of her. There's a card for her in the trailer if you want to sign it."

Em's guilt and nausea resurfaced as she imagined Irma in a hospital bed. They mic'ed up Em and sent her to the tent.

The tent felt like a sauna. The fruits laid out for the challenge to sweat. Cantaloupes, guava, mango, and peaches. Em's eyes fell on a row of pineapples, and she gravitated toward their prickly exteriors.

Their task today was soufflé, a recipe that already flirted with disaster. Change just one ingredient, like the fruit, and it could collapse. Underestimate the quirks of your oven, and it could collapse. Hell, look at a soufflé wrong, and it could collapse.

As she glanced around at the bakers, she wondered who would get the kiss of luck today. Her eyes landed on Chloe, and although Em knew she was a deserving competitor, the thought of watching Chloe win again made her squirm. Four red picnic tables left. One more chance for the top three.

Em nervously adjusted her neck scarf and cradled one of the pineapples in her hand. Something inside her itched. Her mother's words reverberated in her mind again. *It's not just about winning the competition. It's about saving your bakery and your reputation and your craft.*

Em gripped the pineapple, and the thorns pressed into the flesh of her palm. Her nerve endings sang. Her whole body buzzed.

"Stations, bakers!" the director announced.

As Em began her preparations, the cameras loomed. Sweat crawled down her back. She grabbed the largest knife at her table and sliced into the pineapple until its sunny, yellow flesh appeared. Then she diced. She tucked the paring knife into her apron as she brought her cream and milk up to a boil in a pan and beat her eggs whites. Her makeup beaded and trickled down into her scarf.

Before she knew it, the soufflés were in the oven and out and ready. Em eagerly displayed them for the cameras. But her elation turned to panic as she realized everyone was still mixing or baking. This meant her soufflés would have plenty of time to cool—and collapse—before the judges witnessed their perfection. It didn't matter how perfect they were now.

Em felt her throat constricting. "Excuse me. One moment," she told the cameraman. She rushed out of the tent. "Shit. Shit. Sh—" She remembered her microphone was still on. She covered it with her hand.

A voice bellowed through her earpiece. "Everything okay, Em? We're still filming. Gonna need you back here."

Her mind raced. She grappled for an answer then saw the trailer with the restrooms. She ran toward it.

"Bathroom," she hissed into her mic.

She slipped into the handicapped stall and locked the door. Then she wriggled her mic and earpiece off her. They both fell in the empty sink.

Em's mind thrummed as she stared at her reflection, damp with perspiration. By the time she returned to her table, her soufflés would be deflated. She stood no chance at winning with flat soufflés.

With trembling hands, she retrieved the paring knife tucked inside her apron pocket and stared at its gleam in the florescent lights. She hiked her skirt up to her hip, exposing her underwear and the bare, olive sheen of her legs. She pressed the paring knife just below her hip and dug in.

Her jaw gritted as she sawed into her flesh. Her skin peeled back like the skin of an apple. Blood slid down her thigh as she continued slicing, the pain explosive. A low howl escaped her throat.

"Em? Em? Was that you?" The earpiece echoed from the sink basin. Em fumbled with her blood-slicked hands. "Em, answer us. Are you okay in there? Shit. Get the medic."

She lowered her mouth. "I'm fine," she breathed. "Just … uh … stubbed my toe. I'll be out in a minute."

She held the slice of flesh steady onto the counter and diced it in pieces. Then she folded the pieces into her neck scarf and tucked it into her apron pocket. She quickly washed the knife, her hands, and the sink to cover her tracks, then she bandaged the wound with a thick layer of paper towels beneath her skirt.

For a moment, the mere contact between paper towel and open wound gave her shudders. But the nerve endings soon calmed, and her breath regulated. She emerged from the bathroom to find a small crowd waiting, including a medic. Nigel was among them. His arms were folded across his chest, his expression annoyed.

"Why did you take off your mic, Em?" he asked.

She brushed him off. "No one wants to hear me pee, Nigel." She wondered if she looked as pale as she felt. Clammy and unbalanced.

"The agreement is microphones on always, even if you're in the loo. Don't let it happen again, or you'll be disqualified."

A look passed between them that made Em's blood boil. She wasn't about to be dismissed for taking a piss. Not this close to winning the competition.

"Whatever, Nigel. We're contestants. Not prisoners in need of punishment."

Nigel glared but didn't push back. He motioned to one of the crew members. "Let's get back to the set before everyone melts."

When Em returned, her soufflés, as she suspected, had collapsed like wrinkled skins into their ramekins. But other bakers struggled more, with soufflés like liquid lava. No one's was perfect, not even Chloe's. Complaints were mounting as high as the heat. This made Em breathe a sigh of relief.

She waited until she was certain the cameras weren't filming her. Then, with one small, swift move of her scarf, she mixed the pieces of her flesh with the diced pineapples in the food processor. She pulsed until a puree formed and combined sugar, vanilla, and cornstarch.

When judging time came, she marched her soufflés up to the front of the tent, locking eyes with Nigel. They asked her about the pool of pineapple sauce on top, as if it was an attempt to hide the soufflés' collapse. Em said she was sure the flavor would make up for the appearance. Then each of the judges spooned out a bite, dripping with golden, tainted sauce, and lifted it to their lips. They exchanged glances and head nods, even Nigel.

Alice let out a delightful gasp. "The flavor's exceptional, Em."

As Em returned to her table, Chloe mouthed the word "bravo."

Em's soufflés triumphed, but it meant nothing when they announced their decision not to eliminate anyone, given the challenges of the heat and Irma not returning. It was still down to Em, Chloe, Derrek, and another baker, who Em believed should have been sent home. She wasn't unsettled by him, though. She was certain he'd be out the next time.

The remaining bakers gathered in front of a fan and congratulated Em on another win. She could tell their smiles were strained, though, and their compliments were short of enthusiastic.

Before she left, Nigel approached her alone and whispered, "Something spilled on your skirt there."

Her eyes followed his finger downward to her hipbone. The stain was wet and dark and visible through her new blue dress. She instinctively covered it with her hands.

"I must have spilled something when I stubbed my toe in the bathroom. Glad I had the apron to cover it."

Nigel continued to stare down at her hands. "I don't remember seeing it when you came out of the bathroom."

Em's mind raced momentarily, then she regrouped. "If you weren't so focused on my microphone, Nigel, then maybe you would have noticed the stain."

His jaw dropped. Em checked his arm as she stomped past him.

She hoped it would look like anger, the way her pace quickened, the growing redness in her cheeks as she marched to the nearest golf cart. She couldn't let anyone know how much pain she felt. The wound tweaked, nerve endings like live wires, every part of her growing hot.

By the time she arrived back at home, the injury was livid. But she smiled as she dressed her tender flesh, picking flecks of white paper towel out of the newly formed scab.

She smiled because she'd won again today. She smiled because she had been right.

Chapter 15

An eviction notice, plastered to the front door, was not what Em expected to find when she arrived at Sweet Florida Treats on Monday morning. She tore it from the door frame and shuffled inside, pelted by rain. Today was just the first of a week's worth of rain forecasted.

Em combed fingers through her wet hair and put on a pot of coffee even though she doubted customers would visit with all this rain. No orders were scheduled for pickup either. But the coffee would bring her to life or be ready in case anyone braved the weather.

As it percolated, filling the bakery with its nutty, chocolate aroma, Em reopened the notice. Her demeanor soured as she read. Two months of missed payments. Three days until they'd change the locks. She was relieved to find the letter dated for this morning, instead of late Friday. All it would take would be a call to apologize to the landlord, explain her memory lapse during the competition, and cutting a check. But she cursed herself for being so careless, for letting the drama of Bake Across America distract her from something so simple and important as paying the rent.

Em glanced halfheartedly at the red rotary phone. But she knew better. She couldn't speak to her mother again, not after what she'd done this weekend. The wound was running with puss after filming. But careful washing and several punishing splashes of rubbing alcohol late Sunday night finally made the scab close and pucker.

Em picked up the business phone beside the register and fixed the embarrassing oversight with her landlord. The landlord was perturbed but understood after Em explained the filming schedule for the Bake Across America. Em just hoped she hadn't talked it up too much. If the landlord believed she'd have a celebrity baker in this space, there was no telling how high the rent would climb.

With no end to the rain in sight, inventory replenished, and little expectation of sales, Em distracted herself with social media, only to find some damning reviews of Sweet Florida Treats.

Used to be great. Now you can't even tell if they're open.

Weird hours—not what's posted on the door. Better luck getting your cakes at the grocery store.

Em felt the blood drain from her cheeks. Her nearly 5-star business review was dropping each day, all because she wasn't there. She leaned her elbows against the countertop and let her head fall in her hands. Lightning struck outside and with it came a low rumble of thunder.

The bell above the front door chimed, and it squeaked open. Em glanced up.

"Hey," a soft voice said. "That bad, huh?"

It was Chloe, dressed in a bright yellow raincoat on top of a miniskirt and calf-high boots. She lowered her hood and beads of water cascaded onto the welcome mat.

"How did you know?" said Em.

"I'm a social media junkie—and I care about you. I just

happened to look at the reviews last night and saw all the comments." She walked up to the counter. "Sorry, Em. But it'll get better. This is just temporary. When you win this thing and it airs, no one will care about past reviews."

Em gave a short, mocking laugh and busied herself with dusting. "I'm not sure I'm winning. Coffee?"

Chloe nodded her head, and Em poured out the fresh brew. "Why's that?" Chloe asked. "You're killing it in the challenges."

"Well, you've won one now, too. And Derrek's good." Em took a long sip of her coffee. She wanted to say, "Because Nigel hates me," or "I've kinda been cheating, and I'm not sure I'll get away with it much longer." Instead she said, "I don't know. I just have a feeling. Ever since Irma ended up in the hospital, something's been off."

Chloe cradled her coffee mug in her hands. "I'm actually glad to hear that. I thought you hated Irma. But, yeah, we went from fun to super stressed in seconds after she got sick. I don't blame you for feeling off. I do, too."

Em ran her hand across the countertop, deep in thought.

"Actually, I didn't come because of the reviews," Chloe confessed. "I wanted to ask you something."

"You know you can tell me anything," Em replied. A lump formed in her throat as she remembered those words, her mother's words, during their last call.

Chloe sighed sheepishly and glanced around the room. "I don't … I don't know if I can do this show anymore. I'm thinking of not filming this weekend."

"What?" Em's eyes briefly lit up at the thought of her biggest competitor gone. Then she softened. "Oh, honey, why not?"

"I'm not really—" Chloe struggled with the words, "good enough? I should have never applied. I think I made the cut because of some fluke."

Em knew why Chloe had made the cut. She was young and pretty and gave good bakes. But she'd never say that to her. She leaned closer. "Chloe, that's just your imposter syndrome talking. You're the only one in this competition that I'm worried about losing to."

Chloe rolled her eyes. "Did you see my soufflé? It was a wreck."

"Didn't you see everyone's soufflés? Why do you think I drenched mine in pineapple? They couldn't even eliminate someone. It was all so bad!"

"But I'm going to be mortified when that episode airs, Em. No baker will ever hire me again. They won't know me like you, and when they see that soufflé, they won't want to know me." She took another sip of her coffee and lowered her eyes. "Can I come work for you again when you win?"

"*If* I win."

"When you win. It's inevitable. I'm just going to be the pink-haired chick who botched a soufflé then macarons on television."

"Macarons are fickle," Em consoled her. "Macarons are the problem, not you. We'll all be nervous this weekend, even me."

The rain continued to drizzle outside, and Chloe looked so forlorn sitting at the counter. Em got an idea. "Want to go practice? In the back kitchen? I have plenty of almond flour to waste."

Chloe looked both surprised and grateful. "Really?"

"Of course. Look outside. It's not like anyone is visiting the bakery today. Except you, crazy."

Chloe laughed and jumped to her feet.

Although Chloe knew how to make macarons, Em mothered

her with the details, just as she'd always done when Chloe was her employee. She coached Chloe on her mixing, warned her against over-beaten meringue, stood over her shoulder to ensure even piping onto the baking sheet. The first couple batches were failures, as expected. But Chloe perfected hers on the third try.

"What do you plan to fill them with next weekend?" Em asked. "We still have to use Florida fruit somehow."

"Strawberry is a classic. But it's been overused at this point in the competition. I kind of want to try lemon."

"Whatever you choose," Em suggested, "make sure it's the pulp or frozen. If any of these judges are worth their sugar, they'll have it. But they tried to trick us with those pasteurized eggs in the first bake. So I'm not sure I can trust them."

"Agreed. I noticed that trap, too!"

"And a little goes a long way! If you make the recipe too wet, you're doomed."

"I think I'm ready then. Thanks for talking me out of quitting the show."

"I did nothing of the sort. I just made macarons with you."

"Well, then *baking* me out of quitting. It was even more convincing. You really think I have a chance at winning, just like you?"

Em bit her tongue, trying to hide the sudden twinge of regret she felt. "It's anyone's game. Either of us could win."

Even as she said it, her own words came back to haunt her. *I need to win this competition. This bakery is all I have left.*

Chapter 16

Em arrived on set for the semi-final episode, feeling like she'd stepped into an oven. The relentless rain showers fogged up the plastic tent. Her dress clung to her skin. Chloe shuffled over as soon as Em arrived. Chloe's hands were shaking, even though she tried to hide it by clasping them together.

Em cradled Chloe's shoulders. "Are you okay?"

"I can't do this. I can't."

Em scanned to make sure no one was watching. "Walk with me. We'll talk it out."

They went over to the bright red picnic tables. The tent felt so empty, with just half of the stations remaining.

Chloe's breath was rapid and shallow. Em rubbed her back and tried to soothe her nerves. If she couldn't get Chloe to calm down, Chloe would cling to her like icing on a cake. Then she wouldn't be able to enact her plan. Another escape to the bathroom. Another deeper cut. But this time she'd be quick about it, back before the cameras started rolling. She'd even tucked enough gauze and tape inside her bra to dress the wound.

Patrick, the baker she thought should have been eliminated last night, was talking up a cameraman. Derrek was at his station, too, scrolling through and responding to what Em assumed were texts. He glanced up at them but, uninterested, returned his gaze to his phone.

Em expected no less. While Derrek's bakes were great, he'd been a distant peer from the start, preferring not to fraternize. Em wondered what his interviews would sound like when the show aired. Maybe he hated them all or thought himself superior. Maybe he was deeply insecure. It was not her intent to find out anytime soon. He could be eliminated from the competition today for all she cared.

Em gently squeezed Chloe's hands as she rambled on about failing to recreate the perfect macarons at her apartment all week. She hadn't succeeded since their time together at Sweet Florida Treats on Monday, and because of that, she was nervous.

Em suddenly found herself distracted by the layout of her table. Dark blue bowls and standing mixers, red spatulas, fresh gingham-printed linens. All was there. But no knives, not even a small paring knife. Em's eyes widened. She peered over Chloe's shoulder at the other tables. No knives anywhere.

"Did you notice there aren't any knives?" she asked Chloe.

Caught off guard, Chloe frowned. "We don't need knives to bake macarons."

"But we've always had knives, several kinds of knives, whether we needed them or not." Em tightened her grip on Chloe's hands. "Where are the knives?"

"Ouch, Em!"

She dropped Chloe's hands and ran off in search of a crew member. Chloe stared, her mouth agape.

"Hey, where are the knives?" Em demanded of one of the aides. She tried to soften her panic, and with it, her voice. But it was impossible. "We always have knives at the stations."

"You don't need them," said the aide, perplexed. "You're

making macarons today."

This logic infuriated Em. Why did everyone suddenly realize they didn't need knives at their tables? Her jaw clenched, and she was about to scold the aide when she felt Derrek's eyes on her again. This time he was interested, but he pretended not to be by averting his gaze and clearing his throat. But his weight shifted closer. He turned an ear in her direction.

"Fine," Em whispered, more to herself than the aide. "Fine then."

Her mind raced with alternatives but found no solutions. Everything she'd planned next depended on access to a knife or, at a minimum, anything sharp. She couldn't pierce her skin with a rubber spatula. Bowl edges were smooth to the touch. Even if she managed to escape to the bathroom again, what would she find there? A toilet paper roll? The mouth of the sink?

She wanted to scream. Instead, she backed away slowly and returned to her station, refusing to meet Derrek's eyes. Chloe was still confused, but she picked up where she left off when Em returned. Em half-listened as Chloe continued telling her about each disastrous macaron attempt.

Finally, Chloe took a breath.

"The problem was probably your apartment's oven," Em consoled her. "They can be so cheap and unpredictable. That's not what we have here. These ovens are more like the ones at Sweet Florida Treats. Professional. Calibrated. I'm sure you'll do fine."

"You really think so?"

"I'm sure of it, Chloe." She couldn't do this anymore, consoling Chloe when she needed to figure out how to cut herself and get blood in her next bake. "Now, if you'll excuse me, I need the bathroom before we start filming."

Chloe gave Em a big hug then released her.

Em strolled aimlessly around the property in search of something sharp. She even considered going back to her car. Surely there was something in the glove compartment. But there wasn't time.

Just before she tried to sneak into one of the trailers, Nigel found her, and with a perturbed expression, he reminded her it was five minutes before they started filming. Em scowled instead of replying. Still, she knew she shouldn't chance it. She lowered her gaze and followed him back to the tent.

From the back table she chose one of the few fruits left, freeze-dried raspberries. A plan for white chocolate macarons with a raspberry drizzle unfolded in her mind. She'd made a version of the recipe a few times before with her mother.

The tension was high as the bakers waited for the baking to start. As the judges spoke, Derrek tapped his foot, and Patrick waded up the gingham napkins on his tabletop. Chloe played with her pink hair. Each challenge had escalated in its complexity, with macarons their most difficult and unpredictable bake yet.

Em thought her win was guaranteed before she arrived at a set with no knives. Now she questioned if she'd even make it to the finale. Her panic and hysteria rose with each drop of sweat.

Does sweat count? What if I sweat into my batter? But she knew this offering was insufficient. Bakes that won contests, bakes that saved businesses, demanded more of her. Blood must be spilled.

The judges counted down, and the bakers, in unison, rushed to separate their egg whites. If Em was making French macarons in her own kitchen, she'd give the egg whites twenty-four hours to relax in the refrigerator. It improved their elasticity and, therefore, the chances of a perfect whip. She noticed Patrick didn't bother with his scale, preferring to count out egg whites instead of measuring to the gram. *Kiss of death.* She was certain he'd be going home.

But that did nothing to ease her worry. She needed another win. Today would be a dance of intricate steps and long pauses. The humidity was their nemesis again, as the macarons would require even longer rest periods than was normal in a temperature-controlled kitchen.

She again cursed the idiot who decided this season of *Bake Across America* should be filmed under the Florida sun. She was sure it was Nigel. It had to be Nigel. She glared at his back every time sweat fell into her eye.

They processed, sifted, whisked, mixed, folded batter into figure eights, and simmered, each contestant fading as the intense day dragged on. Em filled her pastry bag and piped perfect white circles onto her parchment papers. If she played her timing right, they'd come out of the oven with full centers and ruffled feet, neither overbaked nor crumbly.

For the filling, she made a white chocolate raspberry ganache by grinding down the freeze-dried raspberries and heating heavy cream and white chocolate chips over low heat. She let the mixture cool in the refrigerator while she prepared the raspberry drizzle.

Unlike other syrups, this one had to be extra thin so she could splatter it across the tops of each macaron, artistically, like a Jackson Pollack painting. She wanted to create art. The contrast between the white macarons and bright red syrup would be a visual delight. If she could get it thin enough, it wouldn't soak through and weigh down the macaron shells.

Chloe materialized from the fog of focus, a confident smile on her face. She wiped her hands across her apron, leaving a powdery white residue on her abdomen. She tapped Em on the shoulder. "How's it going?" she whispered. "Need any help? They're about to call time."

Em searched the tent and realized everyone had finished but her. Chloe's lemon macarons sat in perfect rows with perfectly smooth, matte tops. Derrek's tower of red, white, and blue macarons seemed custom-made to match the set. Patrick whined over his mushy macaron shells, as she predicted he would. There was no hope for him since he didn't bother to measure ingredients.

But the idea of losing to the clock instead of Patrick left Em in distress. She was still thinning her raspberry drizzle with water by the spoonful. Her macaron shells already had to go back into the oven another minute or two because they were underbaked. They still weren't cool enough yet to peel off the parchment paper.

She berated herself for focusing more on her bake than the pace of her competition. A cameraman appeared over her shoulder.

She tried to whisper, but she knew the microphone would pick up on the desperation in her voice. She was vulnerable, exposed, and the only one who could help was Chloe.

"Could you fill the macarons the minute they're cooled?" She gulped. "Please?"

"For you, Em, anything."

They fell into the familiar, effortless waltz of a baking team. They'd need an assembly line, like they'd done before at Sweet Florida Treats. But Em didn't need to give instructions. Chloe read her mind with one look. Pipe ganache into one shell.

Cap with another. Splash on the raspberry drizzle. Repeat. Hopefully, they'd beat the clock.

Em grabbed the piping bag and bowl of ganache out of the fridge while Chloe cleared the table of everything but the trays of macaron shells. Then Em heard the whirl of a machine and a pitiful yelp. She turned around to find Chloe cradling a bloody hand. Chloe's eyes, full of fear, met Em's again just before she collapsed on the floor. The producers and medic rushed over. Everyone huddled around Chloe, blocking out Em's view.

As Em surveyed the scene, she pieced together what happened to Chloe. The hand mixer was on the table, still plugged in. She must have forgotten it. A vibrant red coated the whisk, beads of crimson dribbling onto the gingham tablecloth. The trays and parchment paper and tops of most of her white chocolate macarons were doused with wet, red droplets, already soaking in. Em grabbed the trays and moved them and the other ingredients off to the side, away from the unfolding scene.

No one paid Em any attention. No one even asked for her help. They were too fixated on Chloe, who took forever to wake. While they attended to her, Em quietly pulled her macaron shells off the parchment, piped ganache filling into each one, then sprayed just a touch more of raspberry syrup on top, alongside Chloe's blood. There wasn't time, she told herself. She had no choice. The red wooden table already camouflaged the rest of the blood spilled.

After Chloe was bandaged and standing again, they filmed the judging of the macarons. Praise was heavy, from Derrek's Americana theme to Chloe's sensational flavor. Nigel was the only one who raised an eyebrow as Em approached the front of the tent. She could see puzzle pieces of time assemble in his stare, how she wasn't finished before Chloe's accident and now, before him, were perfect macarons. Or was she imagining his suspicion? Maybe no one knew but her.

Nigel bit into white skin of the macaron. She watched it crumble into his mouth. Then Alice and Omar followed. The three judges all fell silent and exchanged a glance.

"Em, this …" Omar paused to take another bite and slowly chew. "This may be your sweetest bake yet."

As she accepted the win, she lit from inside with the hope of taking the entire competition. She imagined the media frenzy that would unfold after this aired. The interviews. The publicity. The possibilities were endless. Sweet Florida Treats could grow into a franchise opportunity, or its products could become staples in every grocery store freezer.

Still, her mother's words echoed, scratching at the back of her brain, coaching her. *You're the only one who can do it.* How far was she willing to go to secure one more win? How much of her would it take?

Chapter 17

Em waited nervously for Chloe to arrive at the bakery on Friday night. The final taping started tomorrow morning, and she wasn't sure she'd be able to sleep. From what Chloe shared on their phone call earlier, she had been asked to film an off-schedule midweek interview to talk about the on-set accident. But their conversation turned to crisis as Chloe, her imposter syndrome already at full tilt, confessed the injury could cost her the show. Chloe's hand was starting to heal, but she needed more time.

Chloe explained that, even though she'd begged, the producers wouldn't extend filming or pause just one more week. After all, they hadn't done it for Irma. Not even Omar, who was a judge. They were on a strict schedule, packing up and moving to the Northeast after they broke down the set this coming Sunday afternoon. The editors were committed to a tight turnaround, too, with a planned release of Season 1 in July. They gently reminded Chloe to review her contract. If she decided not to film the final episode, let them know. It was cold and calculated. Chloe felt blindsided.

Em could empathize with Chloe's struggle, but she couldn't divulge why. Chloe had no clue of the horrors hidden in Em's gloves at the Strawberry Festival back in March, let alone the horrors she'd baked into every one of her victories since.

So while Em spent the week daydreaming of how life would improve after her *Bake Across America* win, Chloe was navigating a recipe with a mutilated hand and a sub-par apartment oven. Her desperation gave Em the chance to offer up Sweet Florida Treats for more practice. She couldn't believe how perfect the timing had been. It was fate.

You'll never have another chance like this, my brave girl. Em licked her lips.

Chloe materialized in the bakery doorway, startling her. She leapt up and unlocked it and invited Chloe inside. In the distance, they heard a low rumble of thunder.

"I'm really glad you called me," Em said. "I was worried about you." She hadn't been, not really. She was so wrapped up in her own vision. But this seemed the appropriate thing to say. "So what's your biggest obstacle right now?"

French croquembouche was the bane of many a baker. Em had made them a few times, by special request, for New Year's Eve parties and the occasional wedding. Although croquembouche was made for celebrations, there was sometimes little celebration in the baking process. Burns of the bake as well as the baker were common. The Florida weather would take their previous bouts with heat and humidity to another level. Choux pastries were already difficult enough—a delicate balance of steam, moisture, technique, and timing. But then they needed to make at least 70 puffs, all uniformly sized, fill them with cream and assemble them into a tower. The final step was a decoration of spun caramel.

The producers knew what they were doing with this final challenge. It was guaranteed to serve drama.

Chloe lifted a heavily bandaged hand to her cheek. "Well, the choux end up burnt and dry, which I'm sure is the oven. But, overall, it's just hard to grip things with this." She sighed and gestured at her hand. "I don't know, Em. Maybe, instead of practicing tonight, you should just give me another coffee and slice of starfruit cake. Maybe I should call the producers and just bow out now."

"That's not the Chloe I know. That's not the Chloe who made it onto *Bake Across America*." She brought Chloe in for a hug. "But I can still get you some of that cake."

She coaxed Chloe to the back kitchen with a slice and some coffee and turned on the dim overhead light.

"What fruit were you going to use?" Em asked.

"I can't decide. Everything ends up so runny, which isn't a great combination with my rock-hard choux."

"Well, is the fruit something that would work well with chocolate?"

"Sure. It's cherries."

"Perfect! Then make the filling chocolate-cherry instead of just cherry," Em suggested. "The chocolate will create a firmer-set pastry cream and help keep the structure of your choux, which will be even more helpful when you go to stack them." Em grabbed a paring knife and larger chef knife off and placed them on the table beside Chloe. "What's your pot situation like at home?"

"Pretty basic. Aluminum."

"That may be one of your problems, too. If the pot's too thin, you could scorch or curdle your pastry cream. The thickening happens so fast. But the professional cooking stuff on set will make all the difference. You just have to keep a close eye on it," she advised.

Em grabbed the eggs, flour, butter, and a sheet of craquelin circles from the refrigerator that she'd already made.

She asked Chloe to walk her through the process she used at home, step-by-step, so she could offer suggestions. Chloe fumbled with the utensils, didn't quite whisk fast enough, and needed to stop more than once to massage a sore wrist. Soon the sound of raindrops cascading onto the roof overtook the sounds of her clumsiness.

"Yikes, it's really pouring out there," said Chloe. The overhead light flickered once, synchronized with the boom of nearby lightning.

"Oh, the cream! The cream!" Em shouted. "Keep whisking. Don't let boil."

Chloe tucked her pink hair behind her ear as she tried to focus harder, revealing a neck vein that pulsed as her frustration grew. Em couldn't help but watch it throb, as if it tried to leap out of her skin. Em's fingertip and hand itched along the old, self-inflicted wounds. The scars along her thigh fluttered.

As Chloe whisked, Em thought of Omar's face, of all the judges' faces. Her sweetest bake yet, they said. Chloe's blood had done that.

You'll never have another chance like this.

Em grabbed the chef's knife.

"Let me help. I'll get this chocolate bar divided for you." Her voice felt high, her throat restricted, but Chloe didn't seem to notice. She turned to Em with a smile of relief and thanks then focused again on whisking her pastry cream.

Em pressed the full weight of her torso into the blade, bearing down on the dark chocolate block until it broke. Once, twice, a third time. Then she pressed a hand into Chloe's back and swiftly drew the knife across Chloe's throat.

Chloe gasped and fell back into Em's arms. Her bandaged

hand tried to stop the blood spewing. But it soaked to red and sputtered onto the table and the floor.

"Shh, shh, shh," Em whispered as Chloe gurgled. "I'm sorry."

She hugged Chloe close, just like they had when she first arrived at the bakery this evening, and slid her body down to the floor. She kneeled down beside her then grabbed a pan to catch the blood leaking from Chloe's neck.

Chloe's body convulsed a few times as the life drained out of her. Em grabbed one of her hands. She stared up, confused, as blood streamed from the corner of her mouth and bubbled along her lips. "Why? Why?" she kept asking. "Why?" Her voice growing fainter.

Em pinched her eyes shut, remembering the fading sound of her mother's voice on the rotary phone line. Chloe's raspy, drowning sobs mimicked her mother's cry, overcome by static.

"I need to win this competition. This bakery is all I have left," Em confessed. Chloe continued to mouth the word *why*, but no sound came out.

Finally, the strain and seizing of Chloe's limbs smoothed to stillness. Her hold on Em's hand relaxed, and her eyes went glossy. Em drug her limp but heavy body over to the walk-in freezer, careful not to upset the pan of blood on the floor. Inside the freezer, she propped Chloe in the corner beside the frozen strawberries. Then she turned away and wrung her stained, cold hands together as she shut the door.

When she returned to the pan of blood, she gathered an ounce into a small vial. She was confident she could slip it up her dress sleeve and pour Chloe's blood into the cream filling tomorrow without raising any suspicions. The rest of the blood she poured into a mason jar and set aside for later.

Eventually, she needed to figure out her plan. Now that she

captured Chloe's blood, and with it the win, there were so many possibilities. What if she was asked to recreate her winning recipe for a cooking show? Or the masses? What if she sold the storefront but manufactured and marketed syrups and jams on her own, keeping her secret hidden? Her imagination twisted with the cost of sustained success. Blood meeting batter, day after day, the demand steadily growing. She'd punish her own veins and flesh for everyday sweetness as much as she could bear. But in times when she couldn't give anymore of herself, she'd exhaust what was left of Chloe's body. At some point, she'd need to find another fresh kill, though. This was inevitable. But maybe her bakes didn't require the blood of a good-natured person. Maybe she could sacrifice a sweet animal instead.

She turned the fan to high and cleaned the bloody surfaces of the kitchen with bleach. Kitchens were made for sterilization. It was gross and smelly, but it wasn't as difficult to get the blood out as she'd expected. Within an hour, every tainted facade looked pristine again. She was glad the bakery was so small and glad one cut was all it took to take down Chloe.

She grabbed the keys and wrapped herself in her raincoat, the night still full of wet, bleak shadows. As she grabbed the front door handle, she thought she heard something. A faint ringing sound, growing louder, echoing from the back kitchen.

Brring-brring! Brring-brring!

Her breath caught in her lungs. She pushed herself out into the rain and locked the door behind her. Then she slowly backed away until the rain drowned out the haunting bell tone. A shudder of relief and dread overcame her.

Chapter 18

Passion fruit had barely come into season, but when Em saw it on the fruit table the next day, she knew it was her choice. They were ripe, with purpled, dimpled skins and soft to the touch. She could already smell the floral, tropical aroma of the pulp and imagined how sweet it would taste mixed with Chloe's blood.

The vial of Chloe's blood pinched into Em's wrist, held there by a hairband and hidden by the long, buttoned sleeve of her dress. A swift pop of the vial top at a strategic moment, and no one would notice her secret ingredient.

She glanced around the set, somewhat sad at the thought of leaving behind the routine of these weekends and the rush of emotions they brought. She checked her watch. One by one, the crew noted Chloe's tardiness. Tense, whispered conversations unfolded.

"She's never late. Someone give her a call."

"I already tried. No answer."

Em eavesdropped and overheard the executive producer confess to the call between her and Chloe last week about her injury and reviewing the contract and letting them know if she wanted to back out.

"I didn't actually think she'd drop out, though. And she didn't seem like the kind to leave us hanging. Keep trying her number," the producer insisted.

Em smiled to herself, only to find Derrek leering in her direction. He shuffled over.

"Where's Chloe? I thought you two knew each other."

"We do. But I don't know where she is."

"Well then, surely you have her cell phone number. Try it," he chastised. "Everyone's looking for her."

Em felt her anger rise, but she had enough foresight to realize this might be a good idea after all. She pulled out her cell phone, making sure Derrek watched her, and found Chloe's number in her contact list. She sent a pithy text. *U ok? U coming?* That should suffice.

Derrek let out an exasperated sigh and crossed his arms as they waited. "What if she's a no show? What if it's just you and me?" he asked.

"Does that make you nervous?"

Derrek rolled his eyes. "No. I'm just concerned for the girl. What if something happened to her? I've spoken to her enough times to know she really wanted to be here. This doesn't make any sense."

A crew member interrupted them. "Hey. We need to pull each of you into the interview space for a few minutes, just in case. Em, we'll take you first."

They sat her down and disclosed what she already knew. After trying to reach Chloe repeatedly, they believed she might not make it to the final episode. Em did the math, figuring the producer who spoke with her on the phone would tape an interview as well. Even if she didn't or framed it in a way that made production appear faultless, the editors would make sure viewers knew Chloe was in a difficult spot. She could either return to the set, slowed and disadvantaged by her injury from last week, or opt out like Irma had done.

Em leaned into the narrative.

"You know Chloe, right? Outside of the competition?" the interviewer asked.

"Yes, she was my first—and last—employee at Sweet Florida Treats. I had to let her go a couple months ago, never knowing we'd both end up on the show together."

"How was she as an employee?"

"Oh, incredibly reliable. She was my best employee. I wish I could have cloned her. It's so out of character for her, what's happening this morning. I've tried to text her, too. But there's been no reply." She paused. "I think I know what's happened…"

The interviewer lifted an eyebrow. "You do?"

"Yes, I think." Em cleared her throat and spun a story about Chloe's growing self-doubt. "She started so strong. I was somewhat concerned I might lose the competition to her. So when she came to me after the soufflé challenge and said she should have never auditioned, that she thought your choosing her as a baker was a mistake, I was shocked."

"What did you tell her?"

Em's lip pulled at the corner, and she shifted in her seat. "I said the only thing a good friend says. You're a rock star, and we'll practice together. So we did. I hope it's not against the rules. But she needed to practice in a place with good equipment and a professional oven—not what she had at her apartment. I let her use the bakery."

"Do you think she got in her head again then? That's the reason she didn't show up today?"

"I don't want to throw her under the bus," Em said. "She's the sweetest girl. But sometimes the sweet ones are the most vulnerable." She couldn't stop fidgeting her hands. She wondered if the camerawoman noticed, if she zoomed in on it. "Look, Chloe called me yesterday, too, with the same concerns. With the injury, the odds were stacked against her. She didn't know what she was going to do." Em knew she had to give the camera something memorable, a clip. "I think the self-doubt crept in, yes. I think it destroyed her. I think that's the reason she's not on set today."

The camerawoman cut, and they sent Em back to the tent. Derrek's interview lasted all of five minutes before he returned, too.

"We're on in five," one of the crew announced.

Derrek turned to Em in disbelief. "So we're really doing this? Without Chloe? Damn everyone showbusiness! Damn you all to hell!"

Em watched his cheeks and neck splotch with red. He spit as he returned to his station. She loved seeing his reserved demeanor crack. Part of her hoped he'd walk off in protest, leaving her crowned the winner. But he stayed, out of shock or desperation, and she watched him squirm and complain through every part of the croquembouche recipe.

Derrek cursed as he mixed the ingredients for his craquelin, sweat as he drove out the dough's moisture, and mumbled to himself as he piped out the dough into one-inch rounds. Then he verbally abused his fruit as he macerated it.

Em and Derrek were neck and neck, but the camera kept fixating on Derrek. So when he reached an emotional boiling point and turned his anger on the cameraman, Em pinched the tip of the vial between her fingers and spilled Chloe's blood into her passion fruit cream. She whipped it through the pale pink filling, darkening it the slightest shade.

Derrek berated himself for burning the caramel on his first try, then again, as he dipped each pastry into the hot syrup and seared his gloved fingertips. His panicked missteps gave Em a cool, calm lead as she made a second bowl of caramel to glue together her cream puff rings onto the plate and stack them into a cone-shaped tower. She pulled threads of caramel around the tower to finish off the piece.

It was flawless. While Derrek delivered a performance, Em believed she delivered perfection. She waited while Derrek sprinted through the final steps, his tower of cream puffs threatening to topple over halfway through stacking. But he managed to wrap the final string of caramel around, just as the judges called time.

Equally stacked and glistening, golden brown, Em and Derrek's croquembouche could have been twins. Em conceded they'd likely get the same marks for appearance. But when it came to taste, she knew she'd triumph.

Each judge plucked a choux pastry from the tops of their towers and bit into it. Both hers and Derrek's rang with the same satisfying crunch. They praised the unique flavor of Em's passion fruit cream and the decadence of Derrek's raspberry and coffee filling.

They broke for a moment to discuss privately, with cameras, of course, then reconvened at the front of the tent.

A grin spread across Alice's face. Omar was stoic, but Em could feel his energy radiate. Em grabbed Derrek's hand and squeezed it. But he didn't squeeze hers back.

Nigel addressed the bakers. "We've seen this win coming for a long time. Week after week, this baker put in the dedication. The bakes may not have always turned out perfect," he laughed, "but today it certainly did. So, now, the winner of the Florida season, the first season of *Bake Across America*, is …"

The judges' eyes flitted between the two contestants as they drew out the seconds.

"Derrek!" all three of the judges shouted.

A pallor spread across Em's features. The tent suddenly became stuffy, the sounds around her muffled. "Derrek?" she whispered. She felt like she'd fallen into a pool of water. "Derrek?"

Derrek dropped her hand and marched up to the judges. Hugs were exchanged all around. One of the cameras locked on Em, but she couldn't break herself from her shock. She thought of the money and time she'd lost, of the sacrifices she'd made, of Chloe's lifeless body sitting in the walk-in freezer.

She froze and stared at the camera lens, seeing herself reflected in it for the first time. She was small and tired and the look on her face was one of hopelessness.

"Anything to say to America, Derrek?" All the cameras turned toward him.

"This win is for Chloe because she couldn't be here. It isn't fair. Everyone loved Chloe. I hope I'll be seeing you again soon. I hope everything's alright."

"Good on ya, Derrek," Nigel said. The cameras zoomed back to Nigel's face. "Now mates, don't forget to join us during season two, where we'll explore what it takes to make a great bake in the state of New Jersey."

Chapter 19

Instead of driving home, Em drove to the bakery after the show wrapped up. She didn't remember how she got there, though, what the traffic was like or if she stopped on red. Her mind was in a fog, her body numb.

When she opened the bakery door, the familiar ting of the bells overhead reverberated through the dark, humid room. Em realized she'd left no lights on, not even one for herself. She placed her keys on the counter and traipsed to the back kitchen, then she found herself frozen, staring at the entrance to the walk-in freezer. She wasn't sure she could ever open the door again. But she had to. She'd left herself with no choice.

Chloe's body was still there in the corner. Of course. She hadn't imagined her betrayal. Chloe's once radiant olive skin looked dull and blueish beneath the too-bright lights. The cut along her neck had hardened from a bright red to a deep maroon. Even the aroma of the bakery, the buttery, sweet scents of cupcakes and pies at her back, was tainted now by the acrid smells of blood and bleach.

Em shivered in the doorway, trapped between two worlds. One of light and one of darkness. One of warmth and one of oppressive cold. She saw the frost clinging to the shelves and felt it biting at her scars. Memories of Chloe smiling and hugging her were punctured with images of Chloe's lifeless eyes. Chloe's words of adoration were pierced with pleads of "Why? Why? Why?" It was like slipping in and out of a nightmare. Em turned and closed the heavy door and leaned her back against it.

The ordinariness of the kitchen threatened to unsettle her. The thrum of the refrigerator fan, the rolling pins, mixing bowls, and spatulas—all there, all acting as if nothing had happened. And all was tainted, reminding her of the violence that had lurked beneath and festered for months.

In the corner, beside the board of reminders, sat the red rotary phone on top of its stool. Em walked over to it and gripped the receiver in her hand. The line filled with a distorted buzz at first, but she willed it, begged it to connect.

Her mother's voice finally surfaced. "Em? I've been thinking about you." Em exhaled, already on the verge of tears, relieved to hear that garbled sound. "It's been so long since we talked. What happened with the rest of the show? Did you have a change of heart?"

Em pushed aside a tear. She was no longer anyone's brave girl. She hadn't been for a long time. She was a monster. A monster driven by ambition, who would sacrifice everything dear to her in pursuit of her dream.

She confessed to everything as her mother sprinkled in utterances of "Ahh" and "Uh-huh" and "I see." She retold the story of the bloody accident and the judges' comments about her sweetest bake yet, how Chloe called in desperation, and she used this to lure her back to the bakery, how the knife felt so light and effortless as it sliced through Chloe's neck, how Chloe's body felt so heavy in her arms as she dragged her to the freezer. Then the shock, the shock that ran through her when they announced Derrek as the winner. Her disbelief. Her agony. Her overwhelming regret.

But when her story ended, the phone line suddenly clicked and fell quiet.

"Mom? Are you there?" Em asked.

Nothing. Not even the sound of static.

The abrupt disconnect left an eerie void where their conversation should have continued. She glanced around the room and saw nothing but herself mirrored in the shiny surfaces. Her blood ran cold.

Em placed the receiver back in its cradle and let go her grip. There was no point in crying out this time. No one was left to hear it but her.

About the Author

Jenna Dietzer is a technology process geek by day and writer by night. She lives in Tampa, Florida with her husband and their fur-kids. When she's not writing, you'll find her chasing down Florida folklore on local ghost tours, decorating way too early for Halloween, or watching documentaries about—what else?—murder. Her work has been featured on The NoSleep Podcast, in Scare Street Night Terrors Vol. 21, Coffin Bell, and a number of indie horror anthologies. If you enjoyed this novella, be sure to check out her debut short story collection, *Fear Her*.

You can connect with me on:

https://www.facebook.com/JennaDietzerAuthor
https://www.instagram.com/jenna.dietzer

Also by Jenna Dietzer

Fear Her
A sorority hopeful is lured into a house of horrors. A city dweller can't shake the mysterious woman who crawls out of her dreams. An inmate discovers the hardest part about being in prison is staying alive. These stories and more tales of motherhood, monsters, and madness dwell in the disquieting pages of Fear Her.